A QUARTER SHORT COMPASSION

T. RENEE

DEDICATION

To My Pride,

Charles, Lamont, Jermaine, Jason, Dwayne, J.T. Damion & Jeffrey; not many in this life can say they've been blessed enough to know a love as ferocious as a lion's heart—I am one of the blessed. Your love means that I have never and will not ever walk alone. I thank you, and I love you. I love you always and forever.

All My Love,
Your Sister (3k for life)
Dark Child

<u>**Compassion:**</u> (Noun) Sympathetic pity and concern for the sufferings or misfortunes of others.

<u>**Dignity:**</u> (Noun) The state or quality of being worthy of honor or respect.

<u>**Integrity:**</u> (Noun) The quality of being honest and having strong moral principles; moral uprightness.

<u>**Pride:**</u> (Noun) A feeling of deep pleasure or satisfaction derived from one's own achievements, the achievements of those with whom one is closely associated, or from qualities or possessions that are widely admired.

Incomparable characteristics that make any man, a man.

PROLOGUE

December 23, 2008

"It looks so good in here, Mr. Otis. Thank you so much for putting everything together."

Chancey's eyes darted around the room in amazement. She truly meant what she said; she thought the room looked great. She saw past the faded blue paint that was peeling off the youth center's poorly plastered walls, beyond the stained and broken ceiling tiles, and she saw through the rusty metal bars that obstructed the view from the window to the dirty street below her.

Otis had gone all out; he'd done the best that he could with the little means that he had to make this evening as special as he possibly could. "Well, it ain't much, Chance, but I did what I could—he deserves it. You *both* deserve it."

"You did more than enough, Mr. Otis. It's perfect, and it is—just enough. I wish you would have told me so that I could have come down and helped you set up."

While leaning on the cane in his right hand, Otis raised his left hand at Chancey and shooed away any idea she may have had that he needed help. "Look now, I may be old, but

I ain't that damn old that I can't hang up a few streamers and put up some balloons."

"I know, I know. But still, I wish you would have let me help."

Otis had done more than just hang up a few streamers and balloons. He had cleaned the floors of the recreation room to the point that they were shining, which considering the age of the floors and the material they were made from, getting a shine on them at all was not an easy thing to do. An outsider may not have noticed his labors, but Chancey was no outsider, and she noticed the floors shining right away; she saw it as soon as she stepped into the room. Getting those floors to shine like that had probably taken up his entire morning and depleted all his strength, but Chancey could see it made him proud to see the gleam beneath his feet, so she quickly dismissed the urge she felt to scold him for doing too much.

That evening, in addition to the buffing the floors until they shined, the long folding table that Otis had set up and meticulously decorated was sparkling too. The table, which was typically reserved for special events like block parties, baby showers, and birthdays, was currently with a bold purple linen cloth, and on top of it lay gold plastic plates and cutlery that reflected softly against the silver *congratulations* decorations that were placed around the table.

Despite his shaky mahogany hand trembling as he pointed at Chancey, Otis was unrelenting in his decision to do things his way and by himself. "The only thing I need your help with is getting a plate together for you, so that you can sit your tail down and eat something."

"Shouldn't we wait for Rome?" Chancey held her breath as she waited for Otis to answer. Waiting would have been the polite thing to do, but she was still hoping he would say no. She loved her brother, but she was hungry and he was late. She couldn't help but lick her lips as she stared at all the aluminum pans that were lined up in the center of the table. All the pans were still steaming hot, and the aromas coming from inside them was making Chancey's mouth water. She didn't have to lift the lids to know what was there. She could smell everything and knew by the aromas that it was all of Rome's favorites: collard greens, red beans and rice, corn bread, fried chicken, candied yams. Despite being small in size, Chancey had an appetite like two fully grown men, and her brother's favorites were also her favorites, and trying to wait on him to arrive tortured her so deeply that a look of pain began to spread across her face.

Chuckling as he shuffled across the floor and shook his head, Otis gave Chancey another dismissive swat with his hand. "Go on, girl, and eat. Rome will be here in a minute."

"He's here now!" Standing in the doorway smiling from ear to ear, Roman walked into the room and headed straight over to Otis, wrapping his arms around the old man.

"Go on now boy, being foolish. Go on and sit down next to your sister and get yourself something to eat before everybody else shows up."

"Thank you, Mr. Otis." Still smiling as he backed away from him, Roman turned his attention to Chancey and raised both eyebrows. "Really, Chance, you were gonna eat my celebration dinner without me?"

"The girl gotta eat!" From across the room with his back turned toward them, Otis waived his index finger in the air, giving Roman a gentle scolding. "And the food ain't just for you anyway, greedy ass. Leave that girl alone and let her eat. You see she hardly weighs anything now. She needs to get some meat on her bones 'fore a stiff wind comes and carries her butt up on out of here."

"I am not that small, Mr. Otis. And where are you going? Come sit down and eat with us."

Chancey smiled at Roman and rolled her eyes. Despite Otis's words, she took a step back and let her brother make his plate first. Once Roman was done, Chancey fixed two plates, one for herself and one for Otis.

"I'm coming. Gimme me a minute. These old legs don't move as fast as they used to."

After over thirty years of being the only maintenance man for the run-down two-story building, it seemed like time had finally caught up to Otis. He'd gotten to the place in his life where you could hear his age in the sound of each exhausted breath he took, and you could see his weariness in the gentle shaking of his hands. But Chancey and Roman gave him strength and so much joy, and whenever he had the opportunity to celebrate them, he took full advantage. "I got a surprise for the two of you."

Once the three of them were all finally seated around the thoughtfully decorated table, they all exhaled with relief and excitement as they smiled at each other. This moment was *home* to them. It was a place in the heart that only they knew how to get to and had found within each other. For years it had been just the three of them. Chancey and Roman had given Otis a purpose, and in return, he had given them solace. Peace often alludes those who seek it, but they had managed to find it within each other, and wherever they were gathered, as long as they were together, they were home.

"It's not much, just a little something for you." Giving a stern nod to each of them as he handed them their gifts, Otis then sat back and contentedly watched as they unwrapped the boxes they'd been given.

"Mr. Otis, this is great. Thank you—for everything. Truly. We wouldn't have made it this far together if it wasn't for you." Roman looked down at the frame he'd unwrapped that held a picture of him, Chancey, and Otis on his high school graduation day.

With the frame held up to her heart, Chancey looked at Otis and smiled. "You big softy. We love you too, Mr. Otis."

"Yeah, yeah, yeah." With his cup of orange soda raised in the air to toast the moment, the space between them went silent, the only sound that could be heard was the sound of bubbles fizzing and popping from Otis's cup as the liquid inside slushed around from the shaking of his strong, yet weary mahogany hand. "Okay now, one of you do the toast."

"I've got it." Roman cleared his throat as he raised his glass and waited for Chancey to raise hers. "Cheers to us for making it through some pretty dark days and coming out all right. The best is yet to come. To brighter days!"

CHAPTER ONE

"911, What is your emergency?"

The distant sound of broken glass crunching on the floor, along with the chaotic sound of radio chatter, filled the quiet space on the phone.

"Hello? Hello, caller, are you there? Hello—911, please state your emergency."

"Uh—hello? Hi. Yes, I'm here" Chancey's slow shaky breath suddenly gave life to what was seemingly a dead conversation.

"Caller, are you in danger? Why are you whispering? What's happening?"

Between each question there was a short pause, an opportunity for a response to be given, but none came. "I'm Judith, can you tell me your name and what's happening to you?"

The long stretches of silence followed by shaky and tense gasps for air indicated to Judith that the woman calling in was either seriously injured or incredibly terrified…or both.

"I'm…I'm in the ceiling."

"The ceiling?" Trying to make sense of the statement, Judith muted the mic on her phone. She briefly mumbled to herself and repeated Chancey's statement as she tried to find reason in what was being told to her. Her silent contemplation didn't last very long, because now not only was Judith concerned, but she was intrigued as well. "A ceiling? Okay. Did you fall? Are you hurt? Why exactly are you in a ceiling?"

Irritation momentarily got the better of Chancey, and it outweighed any anxiety and physical pain she was in. She briefly lost her patience and let out a loud sharp exasperated sigh that seemed to echo through the phone.

"The store where they were shooting. I'm in the ceiling of the store where they were just shooting. I climbed up into the ceiling right before they started shooting, and well—I'd really like to come out now, but the police are still in here and I don't wanna come down and freak anyone out by just all of a sudden dropping out of the sky. 'Cause you know the whole point of me crawling up here was *not* to get shot. So, can you call them? Can you call them and let them know that I'm in the ceiling and I wanna come down, and to please, please, *not* shoot me?"

Judith now understood the situation better and was finally able to relax a little bit. "Okay ma'am, I think we're on the same page now, and I understand why you called in. Don't worry; I will definitely let them know that you're there. Now, were you involved in the shooting? Did you crawl up there to get away from someone you know? Ma'am? Ma'am, what's your name?"

"No! No, I was not involved in the shooting. I climbed up here to get away from the shooting and all of the people with guns. Like I said before, I really wanna come down now." Realizing her attitude had gotten away from her for the second time, Chancey sighed. "Sorry, I didn't mean to snap at you like that, Judith…and it's, Chancey. My name is, Chancey. So, Judith, you think you can help get me down from here now?"

Before Judith had a chance to respond, Chancey was shaken by the sound of a voice coming from directly beneath her, a voice that was calling her name.

"Chancey! Chancey, this is Detective Lorenzo Ducet, where are you? Call out."

The sound of Lorenzo's baritone voice suddenly calling out her name was unnerving, and the acute command for her to show herself was immediately followed by a wave of uncomfortable silence, which panicked her even more. Once she had reclaimed what she could of her nerves, she closed her eyes and took a breath. "Okay, Judith, tell them I'm coming down now. And Judith, thank you."

After she managed to reach her arm around herself and shove her cell phone in her back pocket, she then brought both her arms forward in front of her and began working to try to loosen the ceiling tile closest to her. After briefly struggling to pull the tile up, she finally managed to shake it loose and pull it completely out of its place. Chancey then carefully set the tile aside on the beam closest to her. She'd gotten this far without being shot, and having a random object fall from the ceiling and scare the armed men below her seemed like a bad idea, so she took her time to make sure the tile was level on the beam and as far away from her as she could. After checking the space in front of her one last time to make sure it was clear of any random objects, she shimmied her body forward and carefully peered into the open space. She knew what happened; she had heard the shots and could smell the gunfire—the screams of the victims still echoed in her mind—but her eyes were not ready for what they could now see. The tragedy that lay beneath her was so much more than she expected. Her eyes swelled with tears and her body froze; she was completely horrified.

The store had changed completely in less than an hour. It was no longer the quaint Creole spot that she had stumbled upon earlier that morning; it had become something entirely different. It was more like a grave now—an above-ground mass grave with too much light—and the light was eerie and unwelcoming. Chancey by no means wanted to step into it.

A dozen men and women stood still in the middle of the store. They stood in the middle of broken glass, busted bags of rice, free-flowing beverages and blood; they stood in the middle of unfinished errands, broken promises, and bullet-riddled bodies. Detective Lorenzo Ducet, along with some other first responders who were still on scene, stood in the middle of the carnage below her. All of them had their heads lifted toward the ceiling, and their eyes were all fixed on Chancey.

"Chancey. Chancey, come down now, please."

Again, Lorenzo's voice caught Chancey off guard; only this time, the sound of his voice combined with what she had just seen was all too much, and it was in that moment that she was completely thrown off guard and totally lost her balance.

She'd been lying sideways in the ceiling on one of the rafters, but with the unintentional jerk her body had just made, she leaned too far to the side and fell off the rafter and went crashing down into the aged ceiling tiles beneath her, wholly destroying several pieces and creating a large void that her legs frantically fell through. As the entire lower half of her body dangled from the ceiling, Chancey held on as best she could to the rafter she'd fallen off and tried to pull herself back up.

"Stop swinging, Chancey."

As soon as Chancey's legs came crashing through the ceiling, Lorenzo ran over to her and wrapped a hand around each one of her legs and pushed up as he tried to steady her. "Chancey, I've got you. It's all right; just come down. I won't let you fall."

The sound of Lorenzo's voice annoyed her. It was the sound of his voice that had put her in this position, and she didn't want to rely on him now to help get her out of it. But she also didn't want to fall, so she continued to try and pull herself up.

"Chancey. I know you're scared, but we can't stand here like this all day. You've got to come down. I promise you—I will not drop you. I will not let you fall. Please just trust me and come down." He could finally feel some of the resistance he'd been fighting in Chancey's legs ease, and he could see her torso take several breaths, and as she did, he braced himself for her descent.

Chancey let her body drop, inch by shaky inch. As she lowered herself down, Lorenzo maneuvered his hand so that as her body dropped lower; his hold on her went higher until he finally had a firm grip on her waist.

"Okay, Chancey, now let go."

Calling on all the courage she could and taking one final deep breath, Chancey shut her eyes and let go. Once her feet were firmly on the floor, she looked around at the carnage that she was now in the middle of, and she felt sick. Despite being in the ceiling during the shooting and hearing the screams and cries of pain, she was so focused on getting out of the situation and finding some place to hide that she hadn't really had time to process everything that had transpired. The weight of the catastrophe that she was standing in hit her heart just as her feet hit the ground. Nausea began to creep up the back of her neck, but it didn't have quite enough time to grab her by the throat and take control of her; someone else was currently working on that.

"Sorry, Officer, what did you say?"

"It's Detective, and I said, what were you doing up there? And who are you anyway? Chancey who? What's your last name?" Lorenzo's support for Chancey stopped the moment her feet were on solid ground, and now as she stood there in front of him, he scowled down at her as he spoke.

Lorenzo's sudden aggression was unexpected and unwelcomed. Confused by his attitude toward her, Chancey took a cautious step back, which to her dismay was met with him taking a solid step forward. If the situation wasn't so serious, the movement between the two of them in that moment might have been humorous. Lorenzo stood at 6'4" and towered over Chancey. The height disparity combined with their posturing and body movements, from a distance, it almost looked cartoonish.

Despite Lorenzo's efforts, Chancey maintained enough distance so that she could look at him from an angle but never had to lift her head to see his face, and in doing, so she maintained her ability to stare him down; which she did confidently and without hesitation.

"Morris. Chancey Morris. I came into the shop earlier today. I wasn't here for anything special; I was just looking around. I'm on vacation for God's sake. I was coming out the bathroom, and I heard people screaming and shouting so I went back inside and—and I tried to go out the bathroom window once I heard the first shot, but there's bars on the windows and I couldn't fit through them. So I climbed on the sink and pulled myself into the ceiling. I would have come down that way, but it's not a lot of room up there to turn around and I couldn't crawl backward, so here I am."

After rattling off as much information as she could, Chancey sighed and took a half step back. Unsatisfied with the information, Lorenzo took a full step forward. "What else? You're not telling me something. What you're saying doesn't make any sense. Five people died here today, one of them was an off-duty cop, and somehow out of everyone, including someone trained in crisis, you're the only one to survive this massacre? Well, no, I take that back, you and the shooters."

Lorenzo's dark brown eyes looked as if they were drowning in a sea of red as he looked down at Chancey. Annoyed by her silence, he kicked one of the shelves closest to him before running his fingers down his stubbly jawline. "Where are you visiting from, Ms. Morris?"

"Virginia. I flew in two days ago."

Lorenzo watched as Chancey's eyes searched the room and the faces of the others still in the store, and while she looked around at everyone else there, Lorenzo's gaze never left her face. "And why New Orleans? You missed Mardi Gras, nothing really going on down here at end of March. It's that in-between time where things are slow and quiet."

"Well, I was thinking about relocating, and I've been to the city before, during Mardi Gras, and I had a good time, so I decided to come back and see what it was like on a regular day, when there wasn't *anything going on.*"

Not in the mood to be sassed by the tiny little outsider in front of him, Lorenzo took another step forward and hardened his gaze. "So, what did you see before you climbed into the ceiling? How many shooters were there?"

Suddenly it was like he had just told Sher she only had moments to live. His questions had struck a chord with her but not in the way that he expected. Her eye's filled with despair, and in an effort to console herself, she brought her hand up to her throat and with the tips of her fingers she firmly massaged the lump that was beginning to form there.

"I didn't see anything. I heard shots and screams from the bathroom and I—I just didn't come out. I climbed in the ceiling and waited for it all to stop, and then I called the police."

"I don't believe you, Ms. Morris." Lorenzo sighed, and the frustration and defeat he felt in that moment poured out in his breath like billows of fog over troubled water. "How long will you be in New Orleans? Where can we reach you for follow-up questions?"

"I'm booked at the Shembrey Hotel 'til tomorrow morning. But I honestly don't think I'll be much help to you."

Shaking his head as he scoffed at Chancey, Lorenzo took out his notepad and he rolled his eyes.

"Write down your number."

Irritated by his attitude, Chancey snatched the notepad and scribbled down her cell number. "I don't know why you need my number. I already told you, I didn't see anything."

Lorenzo studied the number on the paper as he took the notepad from Chancey. As he put the pad back into the inside pocket of his blazer, he retrieved a business card and handed it to her. "And I already told you, I don't believe you, Ms. Morris. I don't believe you and I will be in touch."

CHAPTER TWO

"Got anything yet, Ducet?" Detective Israel Saint James stood behind Lorenzo and stared down at his computer screen as he loudly slurped his coffee.

Despite the bright lights, ringing phones, and the sound of fax machines and printers going off, the squad room was as still and as somber as Lorenzo was that morning. He was there, but he wasn't there. Things were happening, yet nothing was happening. It had only been one day since they laid poor Officer Victoria Belgrade to rest. The entire unit mourned her, but the grief that seemed to be weighing Lorenzo down was far greater and heavier than what anyone else seemed to be shouldering.

As Lorenzo moved his attention from the computer screen he'd been staring at blankly for the past hour, he clasped his hands together behind his head and leaned back in his seat. "Nah, Saint James. Nothing yet. There's so much shit to process, it's like, where do you start, ya know?"

"What about the surveillance footage? Has that gone through evidence yet?"

"No, not yet. It's a digital system with a code, and the owner is one of the victims so he ain't saying nothing. And his wife, when she found out what happened, she had a fit and ended up in the hospital. I spoke with her though, and either she never knew the code or she's too upset to remember it. The boys over in tech are working on it though."

Rubbing the bottom of his lip with his thumb as he tapped his coffee cup with his other hand, Israel slowly nodded to himself as he walked over to his desk, which was located just opposite of Lorenzo's. "So, how you been holding up?"

"What do you mean?"

Israel placed his coffee cup down on his desk as he tried to carefully broach the subject. "I mean, how you been doing since—you know?"

"You talking about Victoria?"

"Yes, I'm talking about Victoria. I know you two were close and that you—"

As he hunched his broad shoulders over his desk, Lorenzo let his arms drop down on top of the scattered papers that lay in front of him. "I'm fine. Well, not *fine*, but you know what I mean. Me and Victoria, we been over for years. I just feel bad for her husband and that little boy they just had. It's awful. The whole damn thing is just awful. A terrible shame. But I'm not torn up about it the way you're thinking, and I'm not upset about just her either. A bunch of people who did nothing wrong died that day for no reason. It's a fucking tragedy, it really is. Other than that, I'm all right."

Israel scrunched his face up a little in disbelief; he was going to comment but decided against it. His comment would only start an argument, which he knew in advance would be pointless, and so he let it go and nodded his head in agreement instead. Israel reached over to the corner of his desk and grabbed the box of pastries he'd sat there earlier. "Well, no offense partner, but you look like shit. The shooting happened a week ago, and you don't look like you've showered, shaved, or slept since that day."

Smiling for the first time in days, Lorenzo huffed as he chucked a pen at Israel before leaning back in his seat. "What do you want me to do, eat my feelings like you do all day?"

Pastry still in hand and his lips covered in powdered sugar, all Israel could do was laugh. The white powder stood out strongly against his caramel complexion. There was no hiding from the small bit of truth in Lorenzo's statement. He liked to eat, but it wasn't because he was eating his feelings; eating good food gave him joy. "Hey now, we can't all be gym junkies like you. I may not be as tall and as muscular as you but, the ladies love me, that's all I got to say."

"And you're gonna love them insulin needles if you don't cut back on all that sugar."

As he laughed at his own dig, Lorenzo rubbed the side of his cheeks as he shook his head; it had been days since he laughed like that. So many days had passed since he had even cracked a smile that the feeling of it now almost felt foreign to him. "You're right though. I do have to shave and clean myself up. It's just frustrating, ya know? How the hell does a shooting like that take place in the middle of the day and no one's talking about it and no one saw anything?"

As he wiped the last of the evidence of the pastry from his face, Israel shrugged his shoulders before taking a quick sip of his coffee. "Say, what happened to that one witness? The girl in the ceiling."

As he stood up to stretch, Lorenzo shook his head in irritation and rolled his eyes. "She *claims* she didn't see anything."

"But you don't buy it?"

"Hell no, I don't buy it."

Agitated, Lorenzo walked around to Israel's desk, flipped open the pastry box, and grabbed a cookie. As he leaned against the side of Israel's desk, he scowled down at the cookie in his hand and thought of Chancey and a sudden rage came over him. The cookie in his hand crumbled against the weight of his fist as he stood there silently and remembered the image of her petulant face staring at him. "She's lying. I'm not sure why or what about, but she's lying."

"But her story checked out, didn't it? She was just here on vacation from Virginia? No relatives or known acquaintances in the area, right?"

"Yeah, that checked out. But, she did leave early. She was booked at the hotel for at least another day, but she left the same night as the shooting."

"Can you blame her? Getting shot at while grocery shopping would freak me out too."

After quickly strumming his fingers across Israel's desk, Lorenzo stood up straight and took a deep breath. "It's not that. I can't really explain it. I just know she's lying. There's something she wasn't saying."

Lorenzo shook his head as he walked back to his desk and took his seat. Even as he sat the tension he felt could be seen rolling throughout his body in waves, and with no cookie left to crumble, Lorenzo grabbed a pen from off his desk and began to firmly click it over and over again as he stared across at his partner in obvious frustration. "I did some checking in on her too, and guess what? There's nothing."

Confused, Israel looked down at the napkin in his hand and waited for Lorenzo to say more, but he didn't. "That's a good thing, right?"

The pen in his hand had finally had enough and it snapped. "I don't know. For her—I don't think so. I feel like she's hiding something or hiding from someone, not just in this case but in general, and if she is hiding from someone, then maybe it does relate to this case somehow."

"And if she is?"

And just like that, Lorenzo's tired red eyes were clear and determined. "And if that is the case, well then she's gonna regret ever coming down from that ceiling."

CHAPTER THREE

As sweat dripped down his face and partially obscured his vision, Lorenzo didn't relent in the punches he threw at the bag in front of him. Each inch the bag swung was a step forward he took caging it back in. Each time his fist connected with the bag in front of him—each right was remorse, each left was rage—he unleashed everything he could not say.

"Damn, partner, how long you been here?" Israel cautiously stood off to the side and watched Lorenzo in all his sweaty frustration lay into the swinging bag. "You know the department ain't gonna replace that after you punch a hole in it."

It was clear to Israel that Lorenzo was releasing some pent-up frustration in the squad's gym that day, which normally would have been a good thing. In fact, the department encouraged it—better a bag than a suspect. But there was something about the intensity of the workout that left Israel unsettled. "You wanna talk about it?"

Breathless but still fighting, Lorenzo didn't take his eyes off the bag. "Talk about what?"

Softly chuckling to himself as he strapped on his boxing gloves, Israel shrugged as he tapped his gloved fists together before looking back over at Lorenzo and the punching bag that he wasn't exactly sure in that moment he would actually get a chance to use. "Talk about whatever got you in here drenched in so much sweat it looks like you've taken a shower and forgot to take your clothes off."

"It's May. You know what that means? I'll tell you what that means, Saint James. That means, it's been six weeks." As the words fell from his mouth, the momentum he thought he was losing suddenly picked up again. "Six weeks and nothing. No leads, no anything, just . . . just nothing. How is that possible?"

"You need to calm down before you give yourself a stroke." All gloved up with no bag to hit, Israel put his hands on his hips and stared down at the floor. "Look, we're gonna get 'em. It's just taking a little extra time is all."

Lorenzo scoffed. "*A little extra time*. You and I have closed multiple cases in less than six weeks, and we can't even get a lead on this one." Emotionally defeated and physically exhausted, Lorenzo finally stopped swinging at the bag, grabbed it with both hands, pulled it toward him, and let his sweaty forehead lean against it. Angry but still fired up, Lorenzo shut his eyes and tried to slow his breathing as he tried to process what Israel was saying.

"I know you want there to be a reason, but I hate to break it to you, there's not always a reason. That's why we have the term *random act of violence*. Victoria was just in the wrong place at the wrong time, and the guys who did it . . . you have to face the fact that we might never find them." As Israel stepped up to the bag, he gave Lorenzo a gentle punch on the shoulder. "The random cases are always the hardest to crack. There's no rhyme or reason to them. Opportunity is the only clear motive. No similarities and no red flags."

As he stepped to the side to give Israel room to begin his workout, Lorenzo pointed his gloved hand at Israel as he used his teeth to unwrap the strap on the other hand. After his gloves were off, Lorenzo quickly grabbed the bottom of his shirt and pulled it up to his face to wipe off some of the sweat so he could see Israel clearly. "But see, that is the red flag. This was a little too random. And as far as opportunity goes, opportunity for what? You shot and killed almost half a dozen people and made off with less than a thousand bucks. Who does that?"

"Crackheads."

Lorenzo sucked his teeth at Israel's suggestion. "Nah, your common crackhead ain't gonna shoot an entire store full of people. And anybody looking for a big payday ain't gonna shoot the owner of the store before he opens the safe. We're missing something."

Unable to get into a good rhythm with his punches, Israel stopped and turned to face Lorenzo. "You got a point there. So, no to the crackheads. Well, what about your girl? We know she didn't see anything, but she was in the store the whole time. Maybe she heard something. A name, maybe."

"Maybe. I don't know. I just feel like there's more—like we're missing something."

Pulling back his left hook, Israel glanced at Lorenzo and huffed. "*You're* missing something all right . . . a life. You're missing a life. You're letting this case consume you."

Israel's comment hit Lorenzo's ears hard, and he took a step back in disbelief and irritation. "And what do you suggest I do? You want me to let it go? If it were me, would you just let it go?"

Halted by feelings of shock and insult, Israel grabbed the swinging bag with both hands to steady it. "Are you kidding me right now? Who said anything about letting it go? And fuck you by the way! If anything, God forbid, but if anything ever did happen to you, you know I'd never stop looking for who did it. And furthermore, partner, I never said you should stop looking for Victoria's killer. What I said was, you can't let it consume you. It's a murder, Lorenzo, and yes, this particular victim meant a lot to me and to you, but it doesn't mean shit to the shooter. Just like the murder last week didn't mean shit to that shooter. You can't expect criminals to be different just 'cause the victim changed. They're criminals, and you sitting in here beating up this bag trying to make sense of the senseless ain't gonna do nothing but drive yourself crazy. You need to step away from it for a minute. Go out, have yourself a drink, listen to some music, do something different. Remember the good times you had with Victoria."

While everything Israel said made sense, the rhythm he got into when his gloves hit the bag helped Lorenzo in a way Israel's words could not. Israel's slow, steady rhythm broke his own and gave him a minute to think. Sweat still dripping from his forehead, Lorenzo took a breath and looked down at the floor in front of him as he closed his eyes and continued to listen to the rhythm of Israel punching the bag. He realized in that moment just how different their energies were. Israel was steady and intentional, while his own punches were erratic and off beat. Perhaps Israel was right; perhaps he needed to take a step back and reevaluate his approach.

"Well, all right then." After wiping his sweaty brow with his equally sweaty hand, Lorenzo exhaled and grinned at Israel, who had managed to make his 5'10" stocky body look graceful as he danced around the swinging bag.

"I'm gonna head home and shower. Call me when you're done here and I'll meet you down at the Quarter and we can throw back a few."

"See." Breathless but still not missing a beat, Israel spoke with each punch he took. "Now that's what I'm talking 'bout, partner."

***

"Now this is what I like to see." Israel slapped the bar top as he swiveled in his stool to greet Lorenzo. "'Bout time you got out and had yourself some fun." Turning back toward the bar, he gave a slight wave to the bartender to get her attention. "Hey Shirlene, baby, can we get two double shots of tequila down this way?"

With a wink and a nod of her head, Shirlene poured two large doubles and slid them across the bar top toward Israel. "Anything for you, baby."

Lorenzo fought back the laughter best he could, but his trembling shoulders gave him away. "Really, you and Shirlene? Shirlene's like sixty years old. She's got twenty years on you. You into cougars now?"

"Hey now, you know me and Ms. Shirlene ain't like that. But just so you know, ain't nothing wrong with cougars; I love me some big cats."

"Of course you do, because you have no standards."

"I do have standards; mine are just a little more fluid than yours. And what you bringing up Shirlene for anyway? You got a thing for Shirlene? Think I'm standing in your way or something? 'Cause Shirlene and me, we family, no competition over here. But if you want, I can put in a good word for you; however, I personally don't think you could handle a woman like Shirlene. She could definitely teach you a thing or two though."

After a good laugh and a toast to Lorenzo making it out the house, both men threw back their tequilas and smiled as Shirlene refilled their glasses.

"You know that's probably what you need."

Lorenzo picked up his glass in anticipation of what exactly it was Israel had surmised he needed. Glass in hand, he looked at Israel from the corner of his eye. "And what exactly is it that you think I need?"

"A woman." Israel swiveled his chair around and leaned his back against the bar as he scanned the room for prospects. "You need to find you a good woman, take her home, and let her remind you how good it feels to forget things."

"Forget what?"

"Forget everything. That's what a good woman does. A good woman can make you forget every problem you ever had, every puzzle you couldn't solve, every worry in the world. Ain't that right, Shirlene?" Israel glanced over his shoulder and winked at Shirlene and smiled.

"That's right, baby. Every man needs a good woman. I wish you'd hurry up and find you one too."

"Hey now, Ms. Shirlene. Now, tonight ain't about me, it's about Lorenzo here. We need to find this sad, lonely man someone to make him forget his worries."

"Lorenzo don't need no help finding a woman. Half the women in here would be happy to spend one night with him; they just ain't interested in wasting their time is all. Everybody knows Lorenzo is all work and no play."

"Damn, partner." Israel shook his head as he shoved Lorenzo's shoulder. "You out here breaking hearts and don't even know it." Israel threw his palms up toward Lorenzo, waiting to be offered an explanation. "What we gonna do with you now, partner? That's a bad reputation to be having down here. *All work and no play.* This ain't the city for that kind of unhealthy living."

Lorenzo fixed his eyes on Shirlene as he slid his empty glass back toward her. "You mind getting me a beer, Shirlene? Apparently, I have a reputation to work on tonight. I need to make sure I stay on top of my game."

Lorenzo had moved to New Orleans nine years ago, and the people in the neighborhood knew as much about him now as they knew about him when he first arrived. As charismatic as he was, Lorenzo was a loner, a solitary, mysterious type who kept everyone at arm's length. His wide toothy smile drew people in, but his ambivalence and lack of tact let people know they were not welcomed to stay. He wasn't personable, but he wasn't unfriendly either. The local women who frequented the Quarter flocked to him when he first arrived. He was a tall, polite, educated man with a tan complexion and a bright smile. But as the days rolled into weeks and then into months, which turned to years, Lorenzo's appearance was overshadowed by his personality— rather lack thereof. Eventually, Lorenzo became someone you noticed but never really saw. New Orleans was his home, but he wasn't a local.

After taking a sip of his beer, Lorenzo licked the condensation from his lips and quickly clucked his tongue. "So that's what people saying about me huh, Shirlene? What else they saying?"

In a moment, Shirlene's eyes had turned dark and cold as she silently glanced back at Lorenzo. The silence between them was sharp and sobering.

CHAPTER FOUR

"What are you doing now, girl?" Otis asked. He used the lightweight push broom to pull himself forward across the recreation room floor of the youth center. He shook his head and sighed in disappointment as Chancey approached.

"Nothing, Mr. Otis. I'm not doing nothing. I just came to check in with you, that's all." Chancey grinned at the old man as he paused and rested against the broom and eyed her suspiciously.

"I'm all moved into my new place."

"All what? You don't have nothing, Chancey. Hell, I've got more than you, and Lord knows I ain't got shit, so I know ain't nothing in your place but a bed and a TV. Talkin' 'bout you *all moved in* like you done did something."

Two months had passed since Chancey's trip to New Orleans, and she decided on the plane ride back to DC, that while her life up until that point had been crazy and full of obstacles and misfortune, it was a crazy that she had almost become comfortable with. What happened in New Orleans was a whole different kind of crazy that she didn't want any part of, and so she decided that at the end of the day, if she got to pick her poison—DC it was. She chose DC because to her it made the most sense; if she was going to be on the run and in hiding, her chances were better in DC where she knew where to hide and knew who she was hiding from. DC was the devil she knew better.

She managed to find a small apartment the same day she got back. It was near Adams Morgan in a multilevel townhome in a really nice area. It wasn't much, but it was just enough for her. The apartment was nowhere near any of the places she used to frequent, and it was miles away from where people who lived in the city knew her. The apartment itself was private and somewhat out of the way, but not too far from public transportation, and the ultimate bonus was that the people she was renting from barely spoke English, so they wouldn't be looking to her for any conversation. There would be no comingling of lives or lies or anything else.

"Mm-hmm." Lips pursed together and his eyes shut in defeat, Otis exhaled and sighed. "You know you never told me about what happened down there in Louisiana."

As casually as she could, Chancey sat down on one of the metal folding chairs pushed against the wall. "What do you mean, *what happened?* Nothing happened. New Orleans just ain't for me, so I came back."

Otis quietly resumed shoving the push broom around the room and ignored Chancey. After getting as much done as he intended to do that day, Otis turned his back completely on Chancey and began to make his way toward the exit.

Confused, Chancey hurried to her feet and quickly fell in line next to the old man. "Mr. Otis, what's wrong?"

Aside from his labored breathing and occasional cough, Otis was silent.

"Mr. Otis?" Her anxiety rising with each unanswered plea for a response, Chancey stepped in front of Otis and gently placed both hands on his shoulders. "Mr. Otis, stop.

Look at me please, Mr. Otis, look at me. What's wrong? Why won't you talk to me?"

"I'm old, Chancey. I don't have the time or the patience to be lied to. So, if that's what you're gonna do, you can just go on and leave me alone." Raising his arm and softly patting Chancey's hand that was still on his left shoulder, Otis shook his head as he watched Chancey drop her arms.

"Lie about what, Mr. Otis?"

As he slowly continued his journey toward the exit, with his lips pursed tightly together trying to hold in what little patience he had left, Otis scowled at Chancey. "I asked you what happened down there in Louisiana, and you looked me right in my face and lied. Of all people, you gonna sit here and lie to me? I deserve better than that, and you know it."

Embarrassed but still not ready to betray herself, Chancey threw up her hands in protest. "But Mr. Otis, I didn't—"

"Don't you do it again now!" Rare was the occasion that Otis raised his voice, but when he did, he made you feel as if you were about ten years old and five feet tall. "You may be good at a lot of things, Chancey Elizabeth Morris, but lying has never been one of them. I taught you better than this. Now, either tell me what happened, or go on and take your little ass home, 'cause I don't have time for it."

Embarrassed and defeated, Chancey went back to where she was sitting at the other end of the room, quickly grabbed two metal folding chairs, and brought them to where Otis stood waiting.

"There was a shooting while I was down there. It was at this little grocery store not too far from my hotel. A bunch of people were killed." Knee to knee with Mr. Otis, her head down and her hands in her lap, Chancey took a deep breath and then exhaled slowly and let the story out as she did.

Otis nodded in understanding as Chancey finished up her recollection of events. "So, you the lone survivor? Police must wanna talk to you then, huh?" He didn't need Chancey to answer to know that he was right. "Well, I knew you was running from something." Otis leaned back in his chair to stretch before sitting up and reaching over and giving Chancey's clasped fidgety hands a gentle pat. "I sure wish you would have told me sooner. I could have saved you some time and energy."

With sadness and sympathy in his eyes he looked at Chancey and shook his head. "You can run as fast as you want, Chance, but you'll never outrun the truth. It always catches up with you…and so does fate. You've been here before, and as hard as you tried to run away from the situation, you're back in it, right back where you started."

"Well look at what the alley cat done drug in this morning." Smiling from ear to ear, Israel leaned in his chair with his arms folded in anticipation of the detailed recount of Lorenzo's night after they parted ways. "You feeling like a new man this morning, partner?"

To Lorenzo, Israel looked like a gossipy schoolgirl . Lorenzo had never been the *kiss and tell* type; but Israel, Israel kissed, told, and showed pictures.

At the sight of Lorenzo's less-than-joyous face, Israel jerked forward in his chair sucking his teeth in disapproval. "Oh well, guess it wasn't good then if you don't have nothing to say. I tried to tell you, you should have let Ms. Shirlene set you up."

"Oh yeah, Ms. Shirlene." The idea of Ms. Shirlene— Ms. Still Getting Jiggy at sixty, queen of the black market and occasional bar keep; the idea of someone like Shirlene setting him up on a date brought a smirk to his face. "Let Shirlene set me up—yeah right. You better hope *good old Ms. Shirlene* don't set your ass up."

"Hey now, I can't have you talking about my baby Shirlene like that. Shirlene's a good woman. And just so you know, she knows plenty of *good women*, if you know what I mean." The insinuation from Lorenzo that Shirlene was too old to be living the way she was, was laughable to Israel. Shirlene was in her prime and had been for several years. Despite her appearance and her past, Israel would testify that she was the most decent woman he'd ever met...without question. Shirlene was born in the Bayou and raised there; she made a visit to the Quarter for the first time when she was sixteen and she never left.

She fell in love with the city the first time she stepped foot in it. Something just clicked with her and the Quarter. The city made her feel alive, made her feel things that she never felt at home. The Bayou was tough living. It could be isolating and cold, but with the Quarter, the city had heart and had showed her compassion when she needed it. Israel couldn't be mad at other people who looked at Shirlene and saw her in a different light than he did. To Israel, Shirlene was a decent woman; she just happened to be a felon. To those who didn't know her, Shirlene was an identity thief, who stayed in the company and the confidence of all the *working girls* in the city. And while she'd never been convicted or accused of murder, people knew that to cross Shirlene could cost them their life. But to Israel, Shirlene was love... Shirlene was a decent hardworking woman who had earned the respect of many by means she'd never discuss.

Israel shrugged and shook his head at Lorenzo. "I don't know why you insist on giving Shirlene a hard time. You know she got out the life over two years ago the last time she was released. She makes drinks now not drivers' licenses and checks."

"Yeah, and a pig with some lipstick on it, at the end of the day, is still a pig. A pretty pig—but still a pig." Lorenzo took his freshly poured coffee and walked over to his desk.

His date from last night may have left much to be desired, but each sip of coffee he took from his cup seemed to give him life.

With his hands pressed to either side of his face, Israel looked at Lorenzo and frowned. "I can't believe you just called Ms. Shirlene a pig. A pig though?"

"I didn't call her a pig."

"You kinda did." Shaking his head, Israel took a large gulp of his coffee. Their coffee preferences, much like everything else between the two of them, were very different. Lorenzo drank his coffee straight, no cream, no sugar. Israel's coffee, on the other hand, was like a candy bar in a cup. In addition to the three tablespoons of sugar he added to it, his creamer was also sweetened and flavored with everything from caramel and pumpkin to Almond Joy and sugar cookie. Lorenzo's coffee was a sharp contrast to Israel's, as was their physical appearance, personalities, and opinions. With Lorenzo, everything was black or white; it was right or it was wrong. He was serious in nature and appearance, while Israel was vibrant. Things were never *this way, or that way* for Israel. There was always a space in between; there was always something more to everything for him. And in true Lorenzo fashion, he only saw Shirlene for the criminal the state said she was, but Israel saw so much more.

"Look now, Ms. Shirlene done helped us out a lot. You keep talking 'bout her badly and she ain't gonna help us out no more."

Lorenzo couldn't deny that Shirlene had helped them out in the past on several cases. The woman knew everyone and everything that happened in the Quarter. Initially, he thought Israel was crazy for cozying up to Shirlene and making their friendship public knowledge, but he couldn't deny that their friendship had helped them close some pretty difficult cases. "All right, all right, I'm sorry. I wasn't trying to insult your girl."

Lorenzo could have said more, but he didn't. He and Israel had been down the *Shirlene road* before and it always ended up in an argument. Lorenzo didn't trust Shirlene. The information she gave was good and always checked out, but what bothered Lorenzo was that he never knew how Shirlene got the information. For Lorenzo, Shirlene knew way too much for a woman who claimed to do so little...*just a bartender, my ass.*

"So, what happened with ol' girl you left the bar with last night?" As he waited for Lorenzo to answer, Israel shook off the tension that was building up in his shoulders for the fight he was fully prepared to have in defense of Shirlene's honor.

"What do you mean, what happened?"

Lorenzo's scrunched-up face was too amusing for Israel not to laugh at. In the midst of his laughter, his body convulsed and his candy-like coffee he'd been holding in his hand spilled out all over his desk. "What do you mean, what do I mean? It's been that long that I've got to explain to you how things work?" The small square napkin Israel was attempting to clean up the coffee with proved to be inadequate, but the four steps it would take him to walk back over to the coffee table was not something he wanted to do just then. Fortunately for Israel, Lorenzo seeing the mess and Israel's sad attempt to clean it got the better of him, and before Israel even had to reconsider walking back over to the table, Lorenzo was out of his seat and on his way to get what was needed to clean up the mess.

Slightly annoyed, Lorenzo sighed as he walked back to his desk. As he passed by Israel again, he quickly threw down the stack of napkins onto Israel's desk right next to the almost empty coffee cup. The napkins hit the cup just enough to knock it over again, sending the remainder of the coffee inside flying out and splattering against Israel's pants.

"See there? Karma. That's what you get for laughing so much, chuckles. And believe me, I know a lot better than you do of *how things work*. I could teach you a thing or two."

"You teach me? Teach me what, Lorenzo? You're boring, a recluse, the only exciting thing in your life is this job."

As he turned his chair to face his computer, Lorenzo smiled to himself and shrugged. "I may not be into as much as you, but it doesn't mean I don't have anything going on."

"Oh please—do tell."

"No, sir. I don't kiss and tell, partner, that's your department. I like to keep my work and my personal life sperate."

With his half-assed cleaning job complete, Israel plopped down in his chair, sighing with exhaustion as if he'd just climbed two flights of stairs.

"Anyway, we got work to do. I finally got a chance to really go through that coroner's report again."

Israel scoffed and shook his head as he scrunched up his nose. "We already saw the report, and we already knew before we saw it what it was going to say: *cause of death: homicide, from injuries sustained from multiple gunshot wounds*. I don't understand why they bother doing autopsies when we already know the answer. Waste of damn money if you ask me."

"I didn't."

"Whatever, smart ass, you just let me know if you see anything interesting…and by interesting, I mean something that I didn't already know. And while you're doing that, I'm gonna close out that Powell case." Smiling to himself, Israel thought about leaving the conversation there with his last statement, but smugness got the better of him. "Good thing

Shirlene gave us that tip on this; otherwise, we'd still be chasing our tails trying to track down the suspect."

Being the stubborn man that he was, Lorenzo didn't even blink at Israel's comment. You would have thought he hadn't even heard him, but you'd be a hundred percent wrong; Lorenzo heard Israel loud and clear.

At 11:00 a.m. it was after breakfast, but it was still well before his lunch hour. However, Israel decided to reward himself with an early lunch today for a job well done in closing out his case even earlier than he had anticipated.

"Powell case is closed. What do you say we head down to Mama Ruby's and get something to eat?"

With is arms extended out and both palms placed firmly on his desk, Lorenzo looked over at Israel with an air of satisfaction.

Confused by the delay in response, Israel raised an eyebrow and dramatically scanned the nothingness in front of him. "So . . . Ruby's?"

"No. No Ruby's." Lorenzo gave a quick double tap to the autopsy folder in front of him. "Autopsy . . . that's the only thing on the lunch menu today, brother. Autopsy findings."

"You can't find something that ain't lost, you can't discover something that is already known, and you can't teach me something that I already know. *Cause of death, gunshot wound. Exsanguination, caused by gunshot wound. Catastrophic injury, due to gunshot wound.* It don't matter how you say it, it's all the same damn thing in the end. They all met their end by way of, wait for it . . . *Gunshot wounds.*"

Unimpressed and patiently waiting for Israel to finish his rant, Lorenzo smirked and tapped the folder again. "You finished now? Is it my turn to speak?"

Irritated that he was about to miss an opportunity to slide into Ruby's restaurant during peak hours—that time of day where breakfast shifted into lunch and he could have the best of both worlds, not to be confused with brunch, which he wasn't a fan of. He wasn't a brunch kind of guy. Israel sighed and leaned back in his seat and extended an arm toward Lorenzo, giving him the floor. Israel wasn't really interested at all in whatever it was Lorenzo had to say about the autopsy report, but he figured it was best to just let him get it out so that they could hurry up and get out the station once he was done and be on their way to Ruby's as soon as possible.

"It was a hit. A planned hit."

Israel sucked his teeth as he quickly got up from his chair and grabbed his blazer off the back. "No shit. That's why there were so many people dead on the scene when we got there."

"Nope. The hit was planned for Victoria; everyone else were just causalities. Victoria was the target."

Curious, Israel let his blazer hang by his side as he glanced at his big empty chair. He was still too stubborn to admit defeat and sit back down in. "And how do you know that?"

"It's right here in the autopsy report. Everyone who got shot that day was hit from a distance, and it was multiple shots, like four or five at least per person, and the shots were scattered—likely because they were running away or trying to hide behind something. But Victoria, based on the crime scene information and the information from the coroner, she got shot last and she died last and according to this report. She'd been shot from a distance too like the others, but she took three shots up close and personal. Now, you can say that's just coincidence, but how often do you see somebody take a shot to the temple on accident?"

"Damn." Back in his seat, Israel threw his blazer on the back of his chair and buried his face in his hands as he shook his head.

"I know, right? Over kill. They went there looking for Victoria and everyone else that was there, just shouldn't have been; wrong place, wrong time for them. The rest of the victims were just a distraction to throw us off. This wasn't no robbery. This wasn't no random act of violence. This was a hit." Lorenzo propped his elbows up on his desk as he looked over at Israel. "I may not have found the shooters in all this mess, but I did find their motive for killing all those people—Victoria."

"But she wasn't even on the job when this went down. Who would target Victoria? Everyone loved Vic. Who would want to hurt her?"

"*Who* indeed."

CHAPTER SIX

"You ready, old man?"

"Ready for what?" Otis scowled at Chancey in confusion as he slowly rocked in his recliner.

"What do you mean, *ready for what*? I told you I was taking you out for your birthday."

"I ain't going nowhere with you, girl."

When Chancey initially asked Otis if she could take him out, he hadn't said *no*, which to her meant *yes* because when Otis meant no, Otis said no. And although he hadn't said no when she first asked, Chancey was far from naïve, and she knew before she got to his tiny little apartment in Southwest DC that it would take a great deal of persuasion on her part to get him out of the house.

"Mr. Otis, really? Come on, it's your birthday. You don't want to go out and celebrate?"

"That's right. It's my birthday, and no, I don't want to go out, so just hush up and leave me alone."

Grinning from ear to ear as she usually did when she could see Otis digging in his heels about something, Chancey gazed at Otis with pure admiration before shaking her head and laughing off his gruffness. To Chancey, Otis was an institution—he was her church, her safe place, and her reason for being. For Chancey, Otis was the personification of truth, justice, loyalty, and love. There really weren't too many things she could think of that she wouldn't do for the old man. But Chancey had decided that, that evening she'd be damned if she didn't get the man to celebrate his birthday. Leaving him alone was the one thing that she wouldn't do for him that night.

Otis sat in the far corner of the room quietly rocking in his recliner with his eyes closed. Chancey stood in front of the oak bookshelf opposite of him and smiled silently to herself as she waited for him to open his eyes again. The bookshelf was handmade and old but in great condition. It could have held fifty to sixty books, but Otis wasn't much of a reader; instead, his bookshelf was filled with photos. Shelf after shelf of photos. All six shelves were littered with pictures, and each cheap silver frame had been exceptionally cared for and was sparkling as if it were twenty-four-karat gold. Chancey briefly smiled at the bookshelf before she let her head drop in quiet remembrance. That bookshelf had always stirred up mixed emotions for her. Faces from her past smiling at her with tenderness without any sense of regret. The faces made her heart swell, but her mind couldn't reconcile her hurt with their frozen joy, and so she hung her head and shut her eyes in an effort to quiet her racing mind and broken heart.

Aside from his recliner, the bookshelf, a record player he kept on a small nightstand in the corner, and a small television that only played the news and reruns of 80s classic television, there wasn't much else in the apartment. Otis's photos were his prized possessions, every single one of them—from the people he knew personally to the ones that he never met. In addition to the frames that lined the bookshelf, the walls of his living room were scantily adorned with photos of his favorite musicians and boxers. Their fat cheeks and sweaty brows added to the soul and character in the room. There was something in the simplicity of it all that comforted her. She could feel their hearts by the looks on their faces; there was a humility and an integrity that inspired her, much in the same way Otis inspired her.

Otis was a simple man. He worked for everything he had, and had everything he wanted. Knowing he wanted for nothing didn't stop Chancey from wanting to give the man everything she had.

"Mr. Otis, come on now, it's your 76th birthday. We gotta go out and do something—a movie, dinner—I don't even care what we do, it's your choice, let's just go and do *something*. Aren't you always the one telling me that we gotta take our small victories where we can? This is a victory, Mr. Otis. You turning another year older, it's a victory and we need to go out and celebrate it."

Unmoved by the mini monologue, Otis didn't even attempt to lift an eyelid. "I already told you, I'm not goin' nowhere." Otis stopped rocking and readjusted himself in his recliner before slowly reaching down to the side of the chair and pulling the lever to elevate his feet. "Now, if you wanna do something for me, for *my* birthday, I'll tell you what you can do for me. Go out and get yourself a life and stop worrying about mine."

Having heard the statement more than once before, Chancey was far from bothered by it. "So, that's it then? You got your feet kicked up and you're not budging?"

Of course, she had planned for this. Chancey knew Otis better than she knew the rhythm of her own heart. "Okay. Sit there then. I'll be back in thirty minutes."

***

It had taken longer than thirty minutes, but it was still less than a full hour before Chancey had returned to Otis's apartment. Once inside, she quickly set the bag and box she brought in with her on the kitchen counter and hurried back into the living room. But before he could get fully on his feet, she gave Otis a gentle shove on the shoulder, a silent insistence that he stay put.

"Don't you mess up my kitchen. I just cleaned in there today."

Chancey couldn't help but laugh at the comment and shake her head. "You clean in here every day, Mr. Otis."

A low growling grumble traveled from the living room into the kitchen, and Chancey laughed as it swirled around her ears. But Otis couldn't argue with her about what she had said because it was the truth. Otis couldn't stand mess—metaphorical, physical or conversational—he hated it all and wouldn't have any of it in his house.

"Okay, here we go." Chancey inhaled the mouthwatering aromas coming from the plate she carried in her hands on her way into the living room. After setting the plates on the coffee table, she quickly ran to the closet in the corner of the room and pulled out two TV trays. "Looks good, don't it? I got all your favorites: smothered pork chops, red beans and rice, collard greens, corn bread, and for dessert I picked up a homemade carrot cake."

"Homemade my ass. You went to the store and got that. That's store-bought cake."

Chancey chuckled and shrugged her shoulders in defeat; she knew she set herself up for that one. After she quietly sat down on the blue-and-beige pin-striped sofa, she waited patiently for Otis to take his first bite of food. Once she was satisfied that everything was to his liking, she took a big forkful of collard greens, shoved them in her mouth, and then picked up the tray and set it to the side.

"So, you ready for your gift, old man?"

"What gift?" Hesitant to put his fork down, Otis looked down at his plate and smacked his lips before setting his utensil to the side and looking back at Chancey. "I thought this was the gift. What else did you buy?"

"A life." Chancey smiled as she winked at Otis who looked as confused as he was pleased. "I enrolled in school."

There was no response, no quip, no slapstick statement. Otis was struck completely silent, and Chancey was delighted. As she sat there staring at him, she took pleasure in the pride and surprise on his face. Chancey reached into her back pocket and pulled out a folded envelope. "My class schedule."

Dumbfounded, Otis looked at the envelope then back up at Chancey in pure amazement.

"Mr. Otis, you tryna catch flies with your mouth hanging open like that?"

"You better hush, girl." With his senses returning, Otis quickly grabbed the envelope and unfolded the class schedule. "Well, get the gun! I'll be damned." Otis's eyes sparkled as he looked down at the paper and smiled. "Well, it's about damn time."

Chancey knew Otis would be proud of her for signing up for classes, but she wasn't expecting this level of awe. His reaction had humbled her to the point that she was completely full—mind, body and soul, she was content.

"What you gonna study?"

"Public administration."

"What you gonna do with that?" Just as quickly as the question had fallen from his lips, Otis waved his hand in the air to retract it. "No, I don't even wanna know. Whatever you do with it, it's up to you. You just be sure to do *something*. You're too damn smart not to do something great with yourself. I've been telling you for years not to let your talent go to waste. Never seen a mind as sharp as yours. I'm glad to see you're finally listening."

"Don't worry, I won't let it go to waste, I promise." Chancey sat back up and smiled at Otis. "I already know what I'm gonna do. I'm gonna open a community center. A safe haven for inner city kids."

"You do know that includes dealing with people, right?" Otis's comment was only semi-serious, but the joy he felt in that moment was complete and immense.

"Yes, I know it involves dealing with people." Chancey grinned as she rolled her eyes. "But it's like you say, Mr. Otis, I've gotta do something with my life while I still got one. And another thing, you know me better than anybody, and you know, I've never really lived my life for me. I never had the time, but now it's like, I've got no one to take care of, no one who needs me, and then I thought to myself, maybe someone does need me and maybe I just haven't met them yet. Which brought me back to you and the community center. I decided I'm gonna open my own center and be someone else's *Mr. Otis*. With the exception of course of cooking, cleaning, and fixing things 'cause you know that's just not my thing."

"Lord knows you can't cook! Or clean! Ima pray for you on those two things, and maybe, just maybe, God will be merciful and send you a man who can cook so you don't starve to death when I leave up outta here."

"Yeah, yeah, yeah. Man, or no man, I'll be all right."
"Yes, you will, baby. Yes, indeed you will."
"Happy Birthday, Mr. Otis."
"Yes, Lord it is. A very, very happy birthday indeed."

CHAPTER SEVEN

"Hey, stranger. I ain't seen you in a few days, where you been hiding?" Shirlene leaned over the bar toward Israel and smiled as she watched him sit down.

"I'd never hide from you, Shirlene." As he winked, he offered Shirlene a smile as an apology for his absence. "Just been busy working on a few cases, but I apologize for not stopping by to check in with you."

Shirlene nodded as she grinned back at Israel, swatted the air with her bar rag, and quickly dismissed the apology; it was both accepted and unnecessary. "So, what you drinking tonight?"

Israel sighed as he stretched his arms over his head. "We gonna have to keep it light this evening. I'm still working on a case."

"What case?"

"The corner store shooting. The one with Victoria."

Curiosity and skepticism covered Shirlene's face. "Y'all still working on that?" In general, Shirlene was reluctant to discuss any homicide within the walls of her bar, but she was even more uncomfortable about having a conversation about a cop killing in there. Shirlene quickly turned around away from Israel and headed to the beer fridge on the opposite side of the bar. After she returned, beer in hand, she set the bottle down in front of Israel and popped the cap off. "Look, I know she was one of yours and it's really sad what happened, but how long y'all gonna drag this out? Ain't nobody coming forward to confess they killed a cop, and ain't nobody in their right mind gonna come forward and say they witnessed someone kill a cop. Shit, if they killed the cop what you think gonna happen to the witness?"

Israel had known Shirlene his whole life, so he knew enough to know when something wasn't right, and this evening something wasn't right. In general, Shirlene was unshakeable. She was the type of woman you could get into a high-speed car chase with and have her sitting in the passenger seat next to you, get pulled over by the police, have drugs in her pocket, and she would look you in your face and unflinchingly tell you, "I never met the person driving the car. I walked to the store and you put something in my pockets, 'cause they were empty when I left the house."

Despite knowing who she was and what she was about, Israel wasn't willing to turn away from the subject at hand. "So, you haven't heard anything at all about the shooting?"

"Not a whisper."

Israel gently tapped the bottom of his bottle against the top of the bar and raised his eyebrows at Shirlene.

"What? You don't believe me?"

"Not a word."

"Israel, you know me. You know I would help you if I could, but you're on your own on this one."

When it came to his job, Israel's relationship with Shirlene worked because they had an unspoken understanding with one another, and they both respected it. Shirlene would help Israel where she could as long as it didn't leave her and her business hurt, and Israel made sure Shirlene wasn't hassled and that things around her way in the Quarter stayed calm. Shirlene had reached a period in her life where she never went looking for trouble, and Israel made sure that trouble never found her.

As badly as he wanted to push for more information, he decided he'd let it go. He'd lose a lead any day rather than lose Shirlene; her respect meant more to him than any investigation. "All right Ms. Shirlene, well, what else been going on around here?"

"Nothing much. Been real quiet lately."

"A quiet Quarter . . . Don't know if I like the sound of that." Israel nodded as he took a quick sip from his beer. "Anyway, Shirlene love, I need you to do something else for me, if you don't mind?"

"Need something like what?" Elbow propped on the bar and rag in hand, Shirlene looked at Israel seriously from out the corner of her eye.

"Don't worry, it's not work related . . . not really."

Shirlene let her arm fall and began wiping down the bar as she titled her head to the side, glanced at Israel, and waited for more detail. "What you mean, *not really?*"

"It's Lorenzo."

"Oh Lord." Shaking her head as she turned away from Israel, Shirlene sighed in aggravation before sucking her teeth.

"Hey now, don't do my boy like that. Lorenzo's good people."

"So, you say."

"He is. I mean, he's a little uptight, and he takes some getting used to, but he's good people."

With her body turned but her shoulders expressing everything he couldn't see in her face, Shirlene exhaled a slight chuckle. "So, what's this favor you need for your *friend?*"

"A good woman."

"A woman? Lorenzo? Lorenzo wants *me* to help find him a girl?"

Laughing as he shook his head, Israel stood up and put his hands up in protest. Based on the icy relationship Shirlene and Lorenzo seemed content to maintain with each other, he realized his request must have sounded more like a joke than a favor. "No. Lorenzo don't know I'm asking. I need you to find him a woman without letting him know it was you who found him the woman."

"What? What the hell you talkin' 'bout Israel? Ain't nobody got time for this foolishness. Besides, Lorenzo's a good-looking man. If he wants a woman, he shouldn't have no problem finding one on his own, but I'll tell you what I won't do, I won't be introducing him to any women that I know."

"Oh, come on Shirlene now, give the man a chance. He's been striking out big time lately. This case with Victoria got him stressed all the way out."

Israel knew Shirlene's silence was in fact an answer, and that, that answer was no. There was something between Shirlene and Lorenzo that Israel could never figure out, but he knew something was there, something more than Lorenzo's job and Shirlene's past. "What is it with you two? You really dislike the man that much? You hardly know him. If you gave him a chance you might like him; he might prove you wrong about all the things you been thinking bad about him."

"I don't want to know him. And giving him a chance might prove me right, then what?" Shirlene sighed and put her hands on her hips as she looked down at the sticky bar mat underneath her feet. She searched for the words she could say and tried to keep the ones she couldn't locked away on the other side of her mouth. "Look, Israel, Lorenzo is not our kinda people, and it's not just 'cause he's not from here; it's 'cause he don't fit here . . . he don't belong. New Orleans is a community, we're a family down here, we look out for one another, and Lorenzo is a man without roots—no past and no future. He is tied to nothing and isn't obligated to anyone or anything. I don't trust him. You have to trust him because of your job, but I don't, and I will not."

After changing the subject, Israel changed his mind about limiting himself to one drink. The conversation between him and Shirlene led to two more drinks before he finally made his way out the bar. Instead of heading back to the station, he made his way to the corner store where the shooting took place. Boards now covered the once community friendly little corner store. The owner's widow decided not to reopen. Losing her husband was hard enough, but returning every day to the scene of the crime was more than she could bear. On the inside, aside from the bodies that had been taken away and the blood that had been poorly moped up, the store itself looked very much like it did on the day of the shooting. Glass lay scattered about the grungy tiled floor along with rice, busted chips, candy, melted ice cream, and all the hopes and dreams of the people who died there. It all lay there blanketed by the despair that hung in the air and clung to you when you entered the building.

Slowly and cautiously as if he were trying to avoid stepping on someone's headstone, Israel made his way toward the back of the store to the spot where their only *witness* had crawled out of the ceiling. As he looked up at the gaping hole above him, he shut his eyes and tried to imagine himself in Chancey's place that day in the midst of all the chaos—there but not there, seeing but unseen.

Once several minutes had passed, Israel opened his eyes and looked deeply into the hole as if he could see Chancey's face looking back at him, and he nodded at the nothingness that was there.

"Lorenzo was right; you *do* know something."

Israel had never been one to push people, whereas Lorenzo strongly believed that people had to be made to do the right thing or else they wouldn't. Thinking back to his conversation with Shirlene as he stood there in the midst of what had now become a box of sorrow instead of the neighborhood store that it was intended to be, Israel decided that this time, for this case, he would do things Lorenzo's way. Shirlene was right about Lorenzo. He wasn't their kind of people, he didn't join in on things the way locals did, and no one saw him as family. But Israel lived and breathed New Orleans, and he realized in that moment that Lorenzo had been putting more effort into the case than he had, and in admitting that to himself, he was overcome with embarrassment and sadness. His heart ached and his chest burned as he stood there trying to figure out when he had changed.

When he first joined the force, Israel made himself a promise on the day of his swearing in, that if he ever got jaded, he'd quit. Israel believed in people the same way he believed in God, and his faith in human decency is what made him such a likeable and relatable cop, and now exceptional detective. Lorenzo often confused Israel's optimism and positive attitude for foolishness and clowning around, but truly Israel was all heart and filled with a tremendous amount of grit. The community he worked in loved him and helped him whenever they could, which is why as he stood there below the dark hole in the ceiling he felt like a disgrace. He felt as if he had failed them; he felt as if he'd let his whole community down.

While he stood by his belief that there would always be random acts of violence, that there were threats more terrible than snakes and gators in the city that people had to watch out for, there were also monsters. They were the chill down your spine, the shadows that could kill you, the face you couldn't see. If it hadn't been for his community, Israel would have been dead a long time ago. They saved him in more ways than one. They also taught him that the monsters don't always win. Israel had written the corner store shooting off as a random act of violence, as a case that would never be solved, but now, now he could see the shadows of the monsters moving in the dark, and as he stood there as living proof that they didn't always win, he smiled at the hole in the ceiling knowing they wouldn't this time either. Whether she wanted to or not, Chancey would be that light that brought them out of the dark, he would make sure of it.

CHAPTER EIGHT

There was always a buzz at the office on Monday mornings. As summer neared its end, so did the patience of many of New Orleans' residents. Mondays were never about anything that happened on Monday. Mondays were about Saturday and Sunday. Every detective's desk in the office was filled with files and evidence from events that had transpired over the weekend, every desk except Lorenzo's. Lorenzo's desk, along with Israel's, was quiet and still. Their desks were in the back of the room, the space that was closest to the coffee area, a space that Lorenzo was willing to nearly barter his soul away to get because he believed, rather he hoped, that his choice of working space would help with Israel's productivity. Lorenzo hoped that if Israel had less distance to walk and people to go past to get a cup of coffee throughout their shift that would mean more time at his desk working. Unfortunately for him, Israel had zero interest in fulfilling Lorenzo's hopes and dreams, with the exception being today. Today, Israel was there.

Usually on Monday mornings when he arrived at the office, Lorenzo would spot Israel at another detective's desk with some kind of powdery pastry in his hand as he intently listened to the shenanigans of the night before. However, this Monday, much to Lorenzo's surprise, Israel sat quietly at his desk with coffee in hand. His pastry was there but untouched and off to the side, his hands were clean, and his eyes were glued to his computer screen.

"Hey, partner, what you looking at?"

After giving Lorenzo a quick glance and nod hello, Israel turned his attention back to the computer screen. "Footage of the shooting."

"You think we missed something?"

"No, I wouldn't say we missed something, more like there's something here I think we may need to look into a little deeper."

Lorenzo was intrigued. After quickly putting his coffee down on his desk, he made his way behind Israel to get a glimpse of what he was looking at. "A deeper look at what?"

"Look." Israel quickly cued back the footage and then tapped the bottom of the screen, indicating to Lorenzo to take note of the time being displayed. "Now watch." Israel had cued the footage to a brief interval where there appeared to be a cease fire in the store. There were four dead bodies on the floor when the shooting stopped. "Look at the time, Lorenzo. Now look at Vic. She's talking to one of the shooters."

"You can't see her face; how do you know she's talking to them? Maybe she's just crying and begging for her life."

"Look, she's squatting, so she's clearly not dead. They've stopped shooting, but no one's moving, and look at the time. Almost two minutes pass before they start shooting again and they kill her and the shop owner."

Lorenzo leaned in closer to the screen as if proximity would give him a different angle. "How do you know they're not talking to the shop owner? He's on his knees too. They know he's not dead either."

"Because his head is down and he never lifts it to acknowledge that anyone is speaking to him. No nods yes, no shakes no. They're talking to someone and I'm telling you, they're talking to Vic."

After walking back around to his desk and plopping down in his seat, pen in hand, Lorenzo tapped at the ledge of his desk in confusion. "Okay, so they were talking to Victoria. How does that help us?"

"The witness."

"The witness? You mean the girl from the ceiling?"

"Yes."

"Tried that, remember? Couldn't get anything out of her."

After closing the file of the footage, Israel turned and rested his arms against his desk and looked across at Lorenzo. "I know, but think about it. She said she didn't see anything—a lie? Yes, I think so, but we'll give her that one, and she said she couldn't hear anything because of the shooting and the screaming . . . now that's where we got her. You saw those two minutes of cease fire? It looked pretty damn quiet in there to me, but she didn't come out. You're gonna tell me she's playing possum directly above Vic's head and didn't hear anything? If that's the case, why didn't she call 911 then? Why not call at the first sound of silence?" Israel raised his eyebrows as he readjusted himself in his seat. "No, she didn't call then, she waited; she waited until she could *hear* the shooters leave, until she could hear the voices that were in the store were gone."

After making his point, Israel got up and to make himself another cup of coffee leaving, Lorenzo alone to sit and think about what he had said and all the information that Chancey had likely heard.

In that moment, Lorenzo wasn't sure how he felt. He had always known that he was right and that Chancey was lying. The only difference now was that he could prove Chancey was lying, and now he wasn't the only one who knew that she was. However, proving that Chancey had lied to them still didn't help the case. Chancey was long gone and not likely to return willingly. Now more irritated by Israel's finding than he was intrigued by it, Lorenzo huffed in frustration as he watched Israel sit back down in his seat. "Okay, so we can prove she's lying, so what? She's long gone now and she's not coming back."

"So, we track her down and we ask her again." Israel took a quick sip of his coffee as he pointed at the computer screen. "Then when she lies, we tell her we got proof she knows something. Then if she still won't cooperate, that's when we tell her we'll get a warrant for her arrest for obstruction."

Lorenzo raised an eyebrow as he slowly nodded. He was impressed, but he was more surprised than anything else; he was impressed to say the least. "You want me to file charges against our witness? A witness who some, by the way, may also say is a victim herself. You want me to file paperwork and have her compelled to give her statement?"

"Exactly."

"Get the fuck outta here." Lorenzo was completely taken aback. "So, you're playing hardball now? Since when? And why? What the hell is going on with you today, partner?"

Israel shrugged his broad shoulders as he shook his head and looked at Lorenzo with confusion. "Nothing. What you mean, what's going on? Nothing's going on."

"This is not you, man. In all the years I've known you, I've never seen you take this approach."

"You mean, your approach?"

"Exactly."

He couldn't argue Lorenzo's points. Lorenzo was right. "Well, I tried it my way. She's had more than enough time and opportunity to contact us and do the right thing and tell us what she knows and she hasn't. And this is about more than just Victoria. All of those people in there had someone who loved them, and they just wanna know why this happened, and they wanna make sure it ain't gonna happen again. Knowing *why* it happened won't make things right, but it just might help us find who did it. If we can find out why they did it first. And like I said, it's not just about Vic. The shooters think they got away, left no man behind . . . they think they won. They ain't won nothing yet . . . and they won't."

A sudden shot of exhilaration radiated through Lorenzo's body. "I can respect that. So, I guess we better get to work and track her down."

The entire morning the two worked in silence barely leaving their desk and barely acknowledging any of their colleagues that came close to them for conversation. By twelve that afternoon, neither of them was any closer to finding Chancey than they'd been at eight o'clock that morning.

"You think maybe she gave us a fake name?"

As he leaned back in his seat, Lorenzo shook his head. "No, no she didn't. I made sure to look at her ID that day in the store before we let her go."

"You sure it wasn't a fake? 'Cause I can't find a home address, employer, telephone number, bank account, or anything else that usually pops in the system."

"It looked legit to me, but like I told you before, she looked like she was running from something, and I don't mean the shooting that morning either."

While intently staring at Lorenzo, Israel rubbed his thumb and his index finger together as he bit his bottom lip. "Well, it's always been my experience that the ones who are good at running are always great at hiding."

"Exactly." Rubbing his temples in frustration, Lorenzo shut his eyes and took a deep breath.

"Relax, partner. I have yet to lose a game of hide-and-seek. Don't let this big body fool you. I am the master of this game. Growing up the way I did, I was always running from something, and I always knew where to hide. I'll find her. You have my word on that."

Israel rarely gave his word on anything. He disliked the ease and insincerity that he associated with it. People were always giving their word away without any meaning behind it, but to him, his word was everything and the only thing he truly had to offer, and he never gave it lightly.

CHAPTER NINE

Saturday mornings had always been Israel's *pay it forward* day. While others slept in, he was up early and halfway through his day before others were halfway through their first cup of coffee. After he at his breakfast, he'd go and feed breakfast to others in the community. Israel used his funds and his free time to feed dozens of kids from in and around the Ninth Ward whose parents didn't have the time, the means, or the physicality for them. Israel lent himself each and every week to his community. In addition to helping to feed the kids in the community, he spent his time working with them, motivating them to stay active and product and out the streets. Whether it was working on their sports game, cleaning up the parks, or teaching them to build furniture, whatever it was, Israel worked as hard if not harder at this job than he did the one that paid him.

"Who the hell is it?" Lorenzo threw the covers off of himself and scowled at his open bedroom door as he sat up. He was pissed off and confused as to why and whom would dare bang on his door at eight o'clock in the morning on a Saturday.

"It's Israel, partner. Get your butt up and open the damn door. Day's getting away from you out here. Let's get after it."

After throwing on a pair of basketball shorts over his boxers, Lorenzo stomped down the short hallway to the front door. "What the hell you want so early in the morning?"

"It's almost ten o'clock."

"No, it's not, and it's Saturday. Who shows up at someone's house before noon on a Saturday? The one day I get to sleep in and relax and here you are."

It was more than just the hour and the day of the week; it was more so about the unprecedented situation. For as long as they'd been partners, neither had ever visited the other's home. Aside from the occasional pickup on the sidewalk for a ride to a crime scene when they'd unexpectedly caught a case at the last minute, their home lives were just that, it was theirs, it belonged to them, each one separate. They never got together for backyard BBQs, and they had no shared love of fixing cars. They worked together, and when they were done working, they went home alone. The fact that Israel was there at his home not only caught Lorenzo off guard but left him feeling unnerved and very disoriented, and then when you factored in the hour of the morning and the day of the week, it just made the situation that much more stressful.

Unscathed by the less-than-warm welcome, Israel excitedly followed Lorenzo into the kitchen. Once inside, he opened the file he'd brought with him and began thumbing through papers inside. "Now, I'll admit, it ain't much, but it's more than what we had."

"What is?"

"What I was able to find on this Chancey Morris."

Still trying to shake off the sleep he'd been pulled out of, Lorenzo quickly gulped down a glass of orange juice as he nodded to Israel. "The runner?"

"Yeah, the runner." Taking his seat across from Lorenzo, Israel leaned the file against the edge of the table and then quickly looked up at him, and as he shook his head in confusion, he turned up an empty palm Lorenzo's direction before he returned his attention back to the file. "Looks like she's been running for a while."

Not that he thought Israel needed it, but Lorenzo understood Israel's empty-palm gesture; he'd seen it before and understood it. He'd been told on more than one occasion that he wasn't exactly the most welcoming person, and there was a certain expectation in New Orleans on how to treat a guest in your home. Israel's open empty hand was a reminder that he was a poor host, and so Lorenzo began to brew a pot of coffee so that he could stick a mug in Israel's empty hand.

"So, what did you find?"

"Nothing really. It looks like she was born in South East, Washington, DC. Parents both died when she was young. Looks like Dad was murdered—still unsolved. And she had a brother too . . . he was also murdered—also unsolved."

"Hhmm, seems like death follows her around like a tail on a cat." As he sat back down in his seat, Lorenzo carefully slid the freshly brewed cup of coffee he'd made over to Israel, and with the tips of his fingers he pulled away some of the papers from the file that Israel had laid on the table.

"Any suspects in the dad's or brother's deaths?"

"None that were solid. No witnesses, no motive listed—well not on the brother. Dad had a record so who knows, but other than that, nope, nothing at all."

"Does it say where she was at the time of their deaths?"

Shocked by the question, Israel let the papers in his hand bend backward as he looked over at Lorenzo. "Oh no, you don't think she had something to do with her own family's death, do you?" Clearly the thought hadn't crossed Israel's mind. The disgust on his face made that crystal clear.

"I don't know if she did or didn't. I just think it's odd that a girl that we can't seem to find seems to keep showing up around dead bodies. The only thing these senseless unsolved murders seem to have in common, is her."

As much as Israel hated to admit it, Lorenzo was right. "No." Israel shook his head adamantly as he pushed the paperwork away from him. "I don't think she had nothing to do with that."

"We don't know that she did, or that she didn't."

"No. I'm telling you, she didn't."

"And how would you know? You don't even know her, hell, you can't even find her. You know nothing about this woman."

As he sipped his coffee, Israel shut his eyes and nodded to himself, it was as if he were having a conversation that Lorenzo wasn't privy to, and each time he paused and let his lips linger on the rim of the coffee mug, it was another exchange, a soft whisper between him and his coffee, a moment of shared confidence that Lorenzo wasn't party to. "You're right, I don't know her . . . but you're wrong too. She didn't have nothing to do with it. She's running 'cause she's scared not 'cause she's guilty." When he closed his eyes again, he could see Chancey's face staring back at him through the hole in the ceiling. There was something in her eyes, a sadness that he could relate to, a truth in them that he understood. "No, I don't know her, but—I know her. And I know this much to be true: she ain't have nothing to do with it."

Unimpressed, Lorenzo shrugged his shoulders. "So, what now? Since you know her so well."

"I'm glad you asked." Clearly proud of himself, Israel straightened up in his chair, put his shoulders back, and squared his big broad chest in Lorenzo's direction. "I did a little bit of digging on her brother—I didn't mean that, like that. Anyway, so I did a little *research* on her brother, and he was a real good kid by the way. He was supposed to be going to college on an academic scholarship. Full ride." After quickly shaking off the dismay that was creeping up his spine as he thought about the promising future that had been snuffed out so egregiously, Israel quickly tapped his stubby finger on the pages on the table. "This kid was sharp. He was valedictorian of his class, a straight A student, no rap sheet, no problems."

"Okay. And how does knowing all this help us find his sister?"

"It doesn't."

Lorenzo threw up his hands in frustration, but before he could get a word out, Israel raised his hands halting him.

"So, the brother didn't lead me to Chancey, but he did lead me to some guy named Otis Benjamin."

"Otis Benjamin. Okay, who's he?"

"Not sure how they're related, but outside of Chancey herself, Otis was the only other person listed for the brother as next of kin. School records, hospital emergency contact information, hell even his valedictorian speech . . . there was video of it online. I watched it. On every and anything of importance it was the same two names, Chancey Morris and Otis Benjamin. I figure if anyone knows how to find her, it'll be him."

As he nodded in understanding, Lorenzo tapped his fingers on the kitchen table. "So now we're looking for Otis Benjamin?"

"No. Not looking for him. I already found him. Otis Benjamin runs a community center up in DC. It took me all of five minutes to locate him."

Surprised and confused, but also very excited, Lorenzo jumped to his feet to get his phone. "Shit, Saint James, why didn't you say that when you first got here? Let's call him up."

"Hold on now, slow down a minute."

But Lorenzo didn't want to slow down. In less than a minute he'd left the kitchen and returned to the table with his laptop and cell phone ready to work.

"Lorenzo, brother, hold on a minute."

Phone in hand he stared at Israel with frustrated anticipation, waiting for him to provide the numbers to reach Otis Benjamin. "Wait on what? Give me the number so I can call the man, so that he can tell us how to find Chancey, so that she can finally give us some answers."

"Wait now, let's not jump the gun. Washington DC is way outside our jurisdiction. Let's not rush into something blindly, hoping that it'll work out. Besides, we got some other leads we could be following up on right here first."

Confused and briefly offended, Lorenzo folded his arms across his chest and leaned back in his seat. "What leads?"

"Hey now, don't go getting all emotional over nothing. You ain't missed nothing, and I ain't trying to say you did."

"Then what leads you talking about, 'cause I've gone over every inch of this case for weeks and I couldn't find a thing."

"I know you did, partner. But that's what part of the problem was."

Arms now folded in front of him and resting on the table, Lorenzo sucked his teeth as he let his shoulders fall forward. Turning his head away from Israel and staring at the wall on the other side of the room, Lorenzo rolled his eyes and turned up his nose as he scoffed at the audacity of Israel's last statement. "*Problems?* First there's leads and now there's problems."

Israel frowned as he swatted the air between them as if Lorenzo's feelings were something tangible that he could just shoo away. "Not like that, partner. What I'm saying is, is that everyone at the department was so close to Victoria and loved her so much, no one really dove into who she really was."

"Because we know who she was. She was a good cop, a good friend, and a good mother."

"I ain't arguing that. But if Vic was anybody else, she would have been more than that, we would have looked for more than that. We would have looked past all that."

"What is it exactly that you're trying to say, Saint James? What is it exactly you think you found?"

Israel sighed as he resisted the desire to try and calm Lorenzo down. "What I found is something we all knew this whole time but never paid it any attention, which is Victoria's sister."

"What about her sister?"

"Her sister did a lot of years of hard living out on them streets before Victoria got her to clean herself up. I'm thinking maybe one of her old debts came due or something."

"Seriously? That's your lead? Baby Ruth Ann? Vic's sister who would literally die for her, that's your lead? You think Baby Ruth had something to do with Victoria's murder?

"Hear me out now." Quickly gulping down the last of his coffee, Israel rubbed his hands together as he geared himself up for the reveal of what could be the biggest break in their case. "Baby Ruth was always grateful to Victoria for getting her out of the life, and she loved her sister more than words can say, I won't argue you on that. I believe it too. But Baby Ruth is a party girl to her core. If she would have never gotten jammed up with that car crash, she would have never let Victoria help her in the first place, and she never would have left the life."

"But she did leave."

"Don't mean the life left her. Those boys doing all that time over at Orleans Parish, you think they forgot how Baby Ruth Ann turned on them and took the stand against them? I know damn well they ain't forget, and if they ain't forget, you think their people forgot? Yeah, Victoria got her out the life, but that don't mean that Baby Ruth was ready to go. Vic just happened to put her in a place where she could never go back, not even if she wanted to."

"So, you're saying, Baby Ruth wanted back in the life so bad that she sacrificed her sister to get back in?"

"What I'm saying is, Baby Ruth never wanted to leave the life, even though she knew it might kill her. If it wasn't for Victoria, Baby Ruth probably would have been dead a long time ago; long as she was high, she was happy. Tell me something, when was the last time you seen Baby Ruth Ann smile?"

Less irritated but more confused, Lorenzo looked at Israel and shook his head. With both his arms extended across the table and palms facing upward, Lorenzo fluttered his fingers back and forth in the air as if the connection Israel was trying to make would fall on his fingertips. "I still feel like I'm missing something, Saint James. How does all this tie into Vic's murder?"

Think about it. The money and the drugs Ruth Ann stole—what happened to it? Victoria got her out the life because the people she was messing around with was gonna kill her for stealing from them, but what all happened to what she stole?"

"It went up in the car fire."

"I can't believe that. I don't believe that for a minute."

"Okay, so what do you think happened then?"

Unsure of the answer but confident in his hypothesis, Israel gave a slight shrug as he nodded his head. "Look now, I don't know exactly what happened to the stuff she stole, but I am sure it ain't all go up in that fire. It was all just a little too convenient if you ask me. The car that she was driving full of money and drugs goes up in flames in the middle of nowhere with no witness, and there wasn't no accident that caused the combustion that anyone could see. And all that evidence got turned to ash? I don't think so. Either Baby Ruth got robbed or Victoria got rid of whatever there was to save her baby sister."

As he slowly rolled his fingers across his thigh, Lorenzo thought about it but was still unconvinced that Israel had a case against Baby Ruth. "It was an old car, Israel. That old clunker was ready to burst into flames at any minute. Plus, Baby Ruth was high as a kite that night and half outta her mind trying to speed outta town in a car that was older than her. Wouldn't take much to set that thing on fire driving the way she did."

As he chuckled, Israel nodded his head and raised his eyebrow at Lorenzo. "I can't lie, it really was a perfect storm, but still, no trace of anything on the scene. Not even a blown-away dollar bill?"

"Because it all went up in flames. Everything was in the trunk."

"The car catches fire, *explodes* into flames, and *everything* goes up in flames? Nothing went flying anywhere? No singed or scorched money or drug bags? Who built the damn trunk, Houdini? Sounds a little too perfect to me. Them drugs did not all go up in that fire, I know it, and if you think about it, you know it too. More importantly, them boys Baby Ruth testified against, they know it."

Everything Israel said made sense. Things fly and scatter when they explode. As Lorenzo paced back and forth in his kitchen, he nodded to the internal conversation he was having with himself. He'd been vigorously rubbing his temples as he tried to make sense of everything Israel was saying. Frustrated with himself, he exhaled slowly and rolled his eyes as he came to terms with what Israel had stated earlier in the conversation, which was that he was in fact the problem. He'd looked and missed the forest because of all the trees. "Okay, so you actually do have a lead. But you know what this means, right?"

"What?"

"This means we'd be investigating the family member of a fallen officer and that officer herself. If we're wrong, we're never gonna to be able to show our faces at work ever again."

"I'm not wrong, Lorenzo." As he rose from his seat, Israel pulled out a few pieces of paper from the file that he'd been holding back. "Look at this."

"What is it?"

"It's Victoria's bank statement and beneficiary information. She left it all to Ruth Ann. And before you say, *well that was her sister*, look at the dates. It was changed to Ruth Ann five months before this all went down. Before she changed it, their parents were listed as Victoria's beneficiary. I mean, Baby Ruth was doing good, probably better than she had ever been before, but she wasn't doing that much better for Victoria to make a decision like that."

"So, what are you saying?"

"What I'm saying is the same thing I've already said, I believe Baby Ruth Ann's debt for what she done finally came due, and Victoria's life might have been how she settled up."

CHAPTER TEN

Monday morning at the precinct looked like business as usual. As Lorenzo walked into the office and made his way to his desk, phones were ringing, radio chatter was playing, and Israel was at someone else's desk with a coffee in one hand and a pastry in the other.

"Hey, partner, you think we can get some work done this morning, or you too busy over there flapping them lips of yours?"

Lorenzo had caught him right after he had taken a bite of his donut. Mouth full and unable to speak, Israel shrugged and smiled as best he could as he made his way over to his desk.

"Good morning, good morning." As Lorenzo sat in his chair, he sifted through the stack of files on his desk. "Looks like we got a lot of paperwork to get through today."

Nodding as he sipped his coffee, Israel took his seat and scooted in as close as he could. With his voice lowered and his neck strained forward, he quickly looked around the room to see if anyone was watching. "So, how did it go with Baby Ruth on Sunday?"

"Baby Ruth Ann is still shaken up. I ain't get much out of her. Honestly, when I got there, she looked at me as if she'd seen a ghost."

"She still staying with her mama and daddy over in the Garden District?"

"Yeah, her parents got a house full again. First Baby Ruth Ann moves back in with them and now they got Victoria's baby staying there too. Apparently, her husband was so torn up over her death he said he couldn't take care of the baby, so he left him with Vic's folks before he hauled ass outta town."

"That's sad to hear. They was only married just shy of a year. They was still in that honeymoon phase, just starting their lives together; I know he's gotta be tore up inside. I don't know if I'd just take off and leave my kid. Guess I can't blame him though. God only knows what I would do in his situation." As he sat and thought about it, sucking air between his front teeth, Israel let out a low whistle as he shook his head. "That poor baby. Mama's dead and Daddy's gone and all before he even had a chance to know who they were."

"He'll be all right. Vic's parents are good people, and they know that the whole force is here for them for whatever they need."

"And what about Baby Ruth Ann? You said that she seemed surprised to see you. Surprised good or surprised like *oh shit, they're on to me* surprised?"

"Surprised like, I was there to tell her, her sister was dead—again. I don't know, man. It's like I said, she opened the door and all the blood just drained from her face as soon as she saw me. It was like her heart just stopped."

With his left elbow on his desk and chin in hand, Israel made circles around his desk with his free hand, allowing his index finger to slowly trace and retrace the same area as he silently tried to envision the face Lorenzo was describing to him. "Fine. She was surprised. Then what?"

"Not much." As he stretched back in his seat, Lorenzo extended his arms forward and grunted as he clasped his fingers together and cracked his knuckles. "Well, she couldn't remember much about the day that Victoria found her on the side of the road. She remembered the car being on fire and riding in the ambulance, but that's about it."

"That's bull and you know it." Needing another cup of coffee to help swallow down the frustration that had lodged in the back of his throat, Israel mumbled to himself as he made his way to the table behind him to pour another cup of coffee. He became so distracted by his thoughts that he knocked over the cup that he had just poured. Annoyed by more than just the mess that he made, Israel clenched his fist and looked up at the ceiling. "Goddamn it! It just don't make no sense. It just don't make no God damn sense."

From his desk, Lorenzo silently watched Israel wipe up the coffee and toss out the sopping wet napkins before he stomped back over to his desk and plopped down in his seat.

"You all right, partner?"

"Yeah, I'm fine."

"Look, I know you're upset, we all are, but you can't let it get to you. Baby Ruth Ann was high out of her mind the night that car went up in flames. It's possible the drugs wasn't even in the car. She might have left the money and drugs wherever it was that she got high that night. She was too far gone to accurately remember anything."

"I don't buy that." Averting his attention from Lorenzo to his computer, Israel typed in Ruth Ann's name and began searching for known associates. "Baby Ruth may be a lot of things, but the girl is no damn dummy. She's got more sense than a little bit." As he sighed, he looked back up at Lorenzo who was silently watching him. "The same way you had a feeling about Chancey, I've got one about Baby Ruth. I hate to say it, but I know I'm right about this."

"Gut feeling, huh?"

"Yes."

"Okay then, we follow your gut. You follow this road through, Saint James. I feel it's only fair to warn you, you may not like what you find around the corner."

"And what's that?"

Elbows propped on his desk and his hands in prayer position as his lips rested on the tips of his fingers, Lorenzo let out a sigh. "To Shirlene."

"What does Ms. Shirlene have to do with this?"

"When I spoke to Baby Ruth, she couldn't remember much of anything about that day, but what she did remember was after it was all over and them boys was sentenced to Orleans's Parrish, she went down to Shirlene's bar to have a drink and was told she was no longer welcomed there—or anywhere else in the Quarter."

"So, what's your point?" Confused, Israel shoved his files aside so he could give Lorenzo his full attention. "You've seen snitches get worse than blackballed from the Quarter, and like it or not, Baby Ruth is a snitch and Shirlene . . . Shirlene don't associate with snitches."

"Isn't Shirlene your snitch?"

Somewhat insulted, Israel grabbed the keyboard at his side and began to roughly adjust it to a new resting place on his desk as he tried to calm the anger he was beginning to feel. "Shirlene is not my *snitch*, she's my friend . . . Shirlene my family."

"A friend who gives you information."

"She's a friend who watches my back. She might lead me in the right direction from time to time, or stop me from barking up a wrong tree. She watches out for me. She's good people."

"She's a criminal."

"She's a friend. Shirlene is as loyal as the day is long, and yeah, she's done her share of dirt, but she never did anything to intentionally hurt anybody."

"That you know of." Lorenzo shrugged and looked at Israel as he waited for his rebuttal.

"I still don't see how this leads back to Shirlene. Shirlene don't want Baby Ruth at her bar no more, so what?"

"Well, I wasn't exactly finished."

Almost out of patience, Israel huffed at Lorenzo before rolling his eyes. "So, finish."

Seeing he'd touched a nerve, which he knew he would, Lorenzo nodded and disregarded the abruptness of Israel's statement. "It's not so much that she told Baby Ruth that she wasn't welcomed in the Quarter. It's that she told her she wouldn't be welcomed back *until* she returned the rest of what she stole and those three boys that she testified against were home again."

Still unable to find his way to the conclusion that Lorenzo had thought he'd drawn, Israel frowned as he let his head fall into the palm of his left hand. "Okay—So?"

"So why would Shirlene expect or even assume that Baby Ruth could return money or drugs that we have on file as destroyed in a fire? Shirlene seems to know more about that day than Baby Ruth can even remember. Why does Shirlene think it's possible for Ruth Ann to return money and drugs after the fire, the arrest, the trial—after everything? Shirlene believes that Baby Ruth can still *make things right,* why is that? Shirlene has to know something about that day that we don't know."

Israel's shoulders sagged as he realized Lorenzo did have a point. Shirlene always spoke carefully and chose her words wisely when she spoke to people. If she truly did ask Baby Ruth Ann for something, it was because she believed it was possible that Ruth Ann could give it; otherwise, Shirlene wouldn't have said anything at all.

With both elbows on his desk and his fingers vigorously rubbing the sides of his head, Israel grunted as he shook his head. At this point in the investigation, he knew the right thing to do would be to go and talk to Shirlene, but thinking about doing what was *right* in this situation filled him with all the wrong emotions. Shirlene was more than just a friend to Israel. They shared something more than friendship, more than laughs and recreational interest; they shared a truth, a history that no one but them knew. With words unspoken they understood each other, and they loved each other. Between them there was a bond and a loyalty that couldn't be explained, and Israel was filled with dread and remorse thinking about how he might be challenging that. But he would do it, he would go and talk to Shirlene about Baby Ruth so that Lorenzo wouldn't. He knew the promise he made to Lorenzo. He remembered how he told him he would do whatever it took to close the case, but for Israel, Shirlene was the exception. Shirlene was Israel's line in the sand. He would follow this trail that seemed to lead to Shirlene, but at the end of it, he would stand with her shoulder to shoulder, and heart to heart no matter where the journey took him.

CHAPTER ELEVEN

"You could have dressed up a little, Chancey. Ain't nothing wrong with a little makeup, some jewelry, maybe wear some high heels or something. You always dressed like you ready to fight some damn body."

Shaking his head as he slowly walked away from Chancey, Otis paused briefly and glared over his shoulder at her before throwing his hands up in frustration. "Ugh! Just don't make no sense. As pretty as you are to be alone all the damn time."

"I like being alone, Mr. Otis. I'm not lonely, I swear." As she followed behind him and spoke to the back of his head, Chancey couldn't help but smirk. "Tell me something, Mr. Otis, why is it that little girls are raised to be independent, to rely on themselves so they don't get taken advantage of, but as soon as they come of age, they're told to find someone they can depend on, and to share their lives? Which is it—stand on your own two feet, or jump on someone else's back?"

Finally back at his desk in the far corner of the room by the window, as he sat down on his unbalanced rolling chair, Otis put one finger up with his right hand as he rubbed his leg with is left hand and tried to catch his breath. "It ain't natural is what it is. We wasn't made to go through life alone. Everybody needs *somebody*."

"I already have you, Mr. Otis." With a smile as wide, and as warm as the beaches in Bali, Chancey cocked her head to the side as she sat on the edge of his desk.

"Get off my desk, girl. If you wanna sit your ass down, there's a chair right there in the corner."

He shuffled his feet quickly back and forth and grunted at Chancey's bad manners. Otis gripped the sides of his chair as if they were the only thing stopping him from knocking Chancey in the back of the head. "And you know what I mean too. Stop trying to be so damn smart. I'm old, Chancey, I ain't gonna be around much longer. Sure would be nice to see you happy and settled down with someone before I leave this place."

"And this *date*, this guy you want me to have dinner with tonight, you're hoping that he might be that *somebody?*"

"He just might be, you never know. Give him a chance; he's a good man."

"*A good man.*" Rolling her eyes as she got up from the folding chair and made her way to the window, Chancey sucked her teeth as she rested her arm on the windowsill and peered down at the dimly lit street. "Again, Mr. Otis, I have you and you're the best man I know."

"First of all, young lady, like *I* said, you need to meet someone who you can share your life with. Fall in love, get married, have some babies. And number two, don't use me as a model of a good man; I'm old, I've got more bad days behind me than I got good days ahead of me. I'm what they call *rehabilitated*. Ain't that what they call it? I've been a lot of things in my life; I don't know if *good* was one of them."

Laughing as she looked over her shoulder, Chancey rested her left hand on her hip and raised her eyebrows at

Otis. "Who says you're not a good man? Whoever would say something dumb like that clearly doesn't know you."

"Truth be told, it's you who don't really know me." He leaned his head back and looked at the ceiling, then sighed. The very thought of his past life exhausted him, physically and mentally. "Chancey, I'm a good man *now*, but I'm a good man who has done some very bad things. Not everybody sees me the way you do. Hell, I don't see myself the way you do."

"That's okay, Mr. Otis, *good men* are overrated anyway and apparently, they die young, and—"

"And nothing. That's your problem right there. You're too afraid to live because you're so mad at the dead."

"I'm not mad."

"Yes, you are."

"I am not."

"Chancey, don't you sit in my face and tell me that lie. You've been mad at your father for over a decade, and your mother for almost as long. And Roman . . ." A silence filled the room with the mention of Roman's name. His memory filled their hearts with so much sorrow that it left them both speechless. Otis cleared his throat and cut through the sadness that was beginning to cloak the two of them.

"I'm not mad at anybody, Mr. Otis."

Turning her head back toward the window, Chancey studied the street below. Images of her family filled the empty sidewalk, and she quickly shut her eyes to block them out. As heartache began to fill her chest, determined not to feel the feelings that lingered deep inside her, Chancey stomped her foot, folded her arms, and defiantly looked down at the empty street. "I'm not mad, Mr. Otis. What I am is hungry. This *good man* of yours is late."

"You ain't starving." He leaned back to prop his elbows up on the desk and let out a loud yawn, which he did his best to cut short. "The man is coming here straight from work. Give him a damn minute."

"Where does he work? What does he do?"

"That's something y'all can talk about over dinner."

"Mr. Otis, really?"

Before he could respond, the buzzer for the front door went off. They both hated the sound of it; it sounded like a mixture of a cat dying and a mosquito buzzing. Laughing as he leaned on the desk to help him get onto his feet, Otis stroked his gray beard with his thumb and his forefinger as he paused to take a breath. Once his breathing was steady again, he quickly shuffled toward the entrance. "He's here. Time for you to go."

Halfway across the room, Otis stopped and looked back at Chancey who was still by the window looking down at the street. "Well, come on, girl, what you doing standing there like that for? He's waiting on you."

"So? I've been waiting on him almost half an hour now."

"Chancey, now don't start. He's a good man, he's got a good job, minds his business, stays out of trouble. He's the kind of man you should want in your life. Get your ass out that chair and go on and have dinner with him. You might even have a good time if you stop being so damn mean."

Reluctant but interested Chancey got up and met Otis in the middle of the room.

"Okay, bye. Have a good time. And Chancey . . . be nice!"

"You're not coming downstairs with me to meet him?"

"What the hell I need to go downstairs for? I already know him. And you're a grown woman; you don't need a damn chaperone. No, you go on ahead. I'm gonna shut everything down up here so I can head home. I'll see you later."

"Okay then, old man, I see how it is." Her hands were on her hips as she took one final deep breath before walking away from Otis. Once she was out of his eyesight, and was halfway down the stairs, Chancey let out a soft giggle that filled the corridor. "And I am nice!"

***

"I brought you some leftovers from last night."

Dressed in his beige Saturday slacks and blue button-down shirt, Otis stood at the door to his apartment shaking his head at Chancey. "When I said, *see you later*, I didn't mean the next damn day."

Laughing as she walked past him and made her way to the kitchen, Chancey gave Otis a brief side-eye along the way. "And what is *that* supposed to mean?"

"Uh-huh, you know exactly what it means."

Following behind Chancey, slowly shuffling his feet in his leather house shoes she'd gotten him for Christmas last year, Otis hummed along to the Al Green record he'd put on that morning as he cleaned his apartment.

Leaning against the kitchen counter, still humming, Otis picked at the bags Chancey had brought in. "What's all this?"

"Leftovers from last night."

"Leftovers? It looks like you ordered two or three meals for carry out."

After briefly giving Chancey an eye of disapproval. Otis reached in the bag and began pulling out the Styrofoam containers. "Oh, ribs." He smacked his lips as he pulled out container after container. Otis's eyes got wider and wider with each reveal until the bag was empty, and then he turned his attention back toward Chancey and frowned at her. "What the hell you order all this food for, Chancey? You trying to embarrass me? Ordering all this damn food like you starving or something. You know damn well your ass ain't missed no meals."

As she listened to Otis lecture her, she couldn't help but laugh. She couldn't argue with him; she knew she ordered a ridiculous amount of food the night before. But she did it on purpose.

"Well, he said, *order whatever you want.*"

"I'm sure he didn't mean the whole damn menu, Chancey."

"Well then, he should be more specific next time, shouldn't he?" After grabbing two plates and some utensils and putting them on the counter, Chancey bent down as she searched the refrigerator for something to drink.

Refrigerator wide open with her arms resting on the door, still hunched over and somewhat depressed by what she didn't find, Chancey turned her head to look at Otis who was happily sampling the ribs. "You didn't make any tea, Mr. Otis?"

"'Cause you don't see it, that means I ain't do it?" Still smacking, Otis rolled his eyes as he pointed a finger toward a pot sitting on the stove. "See there? It's sitting right there next to you steeping on the stove."

As she removed the lid from the pot, the odor of fresh mint filled the air. Pouting as she took one last longing look inside the pot before she put the lid back on, Chancey groaned as she let her head sag to the side. "Dang, too hot. Would have been the perfect drink to have with the meal."

"Oh, shut up, you think that tea is perfect with anything. You know what would be perfect with this meal?"

"What?"

"A little bit of the truth."

"Mr. Otis, I told you the truth. The guy was nice and everything. I see why you like him, not sure why you thought I would like him . . . he's boring. Definitely not my type. He just kept going on and on about how he wanted to give back to the community, and about infrastructure and his college years and blah, blah, blah."

He watched Chancey as she moaned on and on about her date while preparing their plates. Otis leaned on the counter with his hands clasped together. His face was completely unmoved by Chancey's angst. "And what's wrong with him wanting to give back to the community?"

"He's not from the community. He don't know nothing about DC."

"Don't mean he can't want to give something to the neighborhood and help out some of the kids around here."

"No, there isn't anything wrong with that, but he's an idealist; he's never been through anything. He can't relate to the people he's trying to help, and he doesn't want to know them. He just wants recognition for saving them, for making their lives *better*. He's judgmental and out of touch. *It takes a village*. You remember telling me that when I was younger? *It takes a village*, you always used to say that. And I get it now, 'cause DC as a whole is a village, and then we have our smaller villages within the village. We're a family here, we look out for each other, and we show up for one another. But this guy, he wants to bulldoze the village and build condos— cold, isolated, and out of reach to the people who already live in the village. The people who live here now won't be able to afford to stay. They'll be standing in the rubble looking at the houses built on top of their homes in the city that they love, in what used to be the village that raised them and their families." Chancey shrugged as she twisted her lips around in ambivalence. "He can't relate to the people he's supposedly trying to help . . . save."

"You mean, *you* can't relate to him."

Plate in his hand as he shuffled to the tiny table in the corner of the kitchen, Otis sighed and shook his head as he sat down. "You don't need to go through something to help somebody out of something, Chance. And speaking of which, what did you get yourself into down there in New Orleans?"

Caught off guard by the shift in conversation, Chancey stopped walking midstep, and stopped chewing midchew. "Nothing. Why?"

"Don't you *nothing* me. A detective down there called the phone last night at the center after you left and wanted to know how to get in touch with you."

Tense and anxious, Chancey slid down slowly into the seat across from Otis and let her plate hit the table a little too hard. "What did you say to him?"

"You know damn well I ain't say shit to him. Told him, I ain't seen you since your brother's funeral." Otis looked down at the succulent set of ribs on his plate to help calm his irritation; good food had a way of making him feel better. As he smacked his lips in anticipation of taking a bite, he quickly clenched his fists together to restrain himself before looking back over at Chancey.

"What the hell happened down there, Chancey? Why is a detective in New Orleans calling all the way up to DC looking for you?"

Before she could answer, Otis let his fork drop and hit his plate so he could free his hand and point one serious finger in Chancey's direction. "And don't you lie to me, girl."

Her appetite ruined and her mouth as dry as cotton balls, she stared back at him paralyzed.

"Ugh."

Otis shook his head as he sighed and waited for Chancey to get her thoughts together. "How trouble finds you, I just don't know . . . but trouble got you in its sights again, and before it gets up here to DC, you better tell me what happened so we can try and fix it. You better tell me the *whole* truth this time. You know I'm here for you, Chance, you're not alone. You are never alone."

Smiling back at Otis, Chancey found peace in his words. They were the same words he'd said to her and her brother, Roman, when their mother passed away. She went to Otis the day her mother died. He lived four blocks away from them back then, but that day, the walk to his house, those four blocks, felt like ten. By the time she got to Otis's front door, her mind had spiraled out of control as she thought about the *what ifs* and her new reality. She was an orphan. Her and her brother were orphans. But that day when Otis opened the door and saw her, he knelt down, took her face softly into his hands, and it was as if he had heard all the words she had not said and somehow managed to take on some of the worry she had inside of herself. He held her face in his own hands, and then he looked at her and told her, *"We're gonna fix it. You're gonna tell me what happened, and we're gonna fix it. I'm here for you, Chance. You are not alone."*

CHAPTER TWELVE

Entering Shirlene's on Thursday afternoon, it was the time of day where everything and nothing was happening all that the same time. But this afternoon was unlike any other before it. Israel's body tensed and screamed in pain as he walked into the bar that afternoon. He was not walking into Shirlene's as Israel that afternoon; that day he walked in as Detective Saint James, and it felt wrong. It felt painfully wrong.

In the dimly lit bar that reeked of sweat and bourbon, Israel felt as if he were the one bringing in the dirt and darkness. He felt like a criminal.

"Israel, baby, what you doing here?" Shirlene frowned as she watched Israel slowly approach her. "You look like you need a drink. Everything okay?"

After she finished drying the glass in her hand, Shirlene reached down into the cooler in front of her, grabbed a frosty beer glass, and filled it to the brim. "Here you go, love, drink up."

With his hand wrapped around the frosty mug and the sound of the foam on top of the glass softly crackling as it settled, Israel stared down into the mug and silently watched the bubbles fizzle and burst as he reconsidered his actions and questioned his integrity.

Sensing his distress, Shirlene leaned over the bar and studied his face. "What's wrong with you? Tough day at work?"

Yes, work was the problem, but at the same time, it wasn't. For Israel, this wasn't a simple yes or no question Shirlene had placed before him. In fact, it was Shirlene herself that was, and was not, the problem. "Ah hell, might as well get on with it." Taking a breath instead of a gulp of beer, Israel exhaled deeply as he rubbed his hands together and braced himself for the conversation ahead.

"I've gotta question you about some things, Shirlene."

"*You* gotta question *me?*"

"Yes, ma'am, I do."

Shirlene winced at the response as she looked across at Israel and nodded. "Go ahead then, let the questioning begin."

"You know Baby Ruth? I mean, Ruth Anne, Victoria's little sister?"

"Yes, I know Baby Ruth. And you know I know Baby Ruth."

It didn't take long for Shirlene to go from stunned and defensive to irritated and insulted. As she turned her back on him, it was like the entire bar could feel the shift in Shirlene's mood. As tension rose in her shoulders, she clucked her tongue, which seemed to release a wave of frustration that echoed in the air. The two day-drinkers who had been sitting at the end of the bar having a friendly conversation gathered their things and left. The up-tempo jazz that had been playing switched to something more melancholy and ominous. The room seemed darker and colder than it had ever felt before.

"Do you know anything about Baby Ruth's car going up in flames when she was trying to leave town two years back?"

"What would I know about that? It's not like I was there. You probably know as much as I do."

Quickly clearing his throat, as he uncomfortably adjusted himself in his seat, Israel rubbed his clammy hands on his pants. "Now, that's not the truth, Shirlene. Baby Ruth says she came to see you after it all went down. She says y'all talked and you put her out the Quarter."

"Is that what she's saying?"

"Yes, ma'am, that's what she's saying. So, what did you talk about? What did y'all talk about when she tried to leave town?"

Emotionally, Shirlene had moved past defensive, and now she was angry. Now she was pissed off and indignant. After slamming the cooler door shut and snatching up her bar rag, Shirlene began to vigorously wipe down the already spotless bar top. "I don't know if you remember this or not, *Detective*, but back then, Baby Ruth wasn't nothing but a crackhead always looking for a fix. Now, I don't know what the girl told you, but I don't know nothing about that night except that the girl tried to leave and ain't make it too far."

"Shirle—"

"No, Israel. I don't know why it is you questioning me about Baby Ruth and about when she tried to leave. I assume it got something to do with her sister's murder, but I'm telling you now to let well enough alone. I'm sorry about your friend, Israel, but you traveling down a road that ain't gonna lead you nowhere good. Let it alone."

In that moment, Israel knew Shirlene knew more than she was saying. The fact that she knew something is not what troubled him. Israel knew that Shirlene always knew more than she said, but what was bothering him was the things not being said. This time, those unspoken words involved Shirlene, and it wasn't anger he felt toward her; it was worry he felt for her.

"Lorenzo is not gonna let this one go, Shirlene."

Seeing the man before her and the concern in his eyes, Shirlene began to soften and relax her shoulders. She could hear the worry in Israel's voice, and it gave the words he'd previously spoken a different meaning; it put things in a different light for her. She realized Israel hadn't brought up Lorenzo as a threat; he had brought him up as a caution. Israel had come to her so that no one else would. Slowly, Shirlene leaned across the bar until she was almost nose to nose with Israel, and without hesitation, she looked him in the eye and gave him a firm nod. "Let him come."

Israel picked up his beer, took a sip, and nodded.

CHAPTER THIRTEEN

"Lawd—there's a storm coming."

Otis sighed and shook his head. He knew everything Chancey had told him was the truth, and he also knew that for her, knowing what she knew was dangerous.

"They're not gonna let this go, Chance." They're not ever gonna let this go. They can't."

"They will, Mr. Otis. They just need some more time. Once some more time passes and they see that I haven't said anything, they'll let it go. They'll let it go and leave me alone. I made it this far, didn't I? It's like when my father died; they left me alone. But they know I know who did it, and they know I know why they did it, but still, they left me alone."

The light in the kitchen illuminated the lie resting on Chancey's lips. Her mouth moved without conviction, and her eyes darkened with the disbelief of the words she spoke.

"We both know better than that, Chancey."

Like Otis, Chancey's father was a felon. He was a good man who just so happened to be a criminal. He was always on the right side of wrong. His means always justified his ends. He was a fighter, and he raised his kids to be fighters, to never back down. He was sent to prison when Chancey was three and didn't get back home to her until she was seven. The first thing he said to her when he saw her was, *I'm sorry.* He apologized to her for having to be stuck with a man like him as her father.

He apologized to her because for her, life would be harder because of him, but he swore he would prepare her for it and he ensured her that anything in this life worth having was worth fighting for. Then when he was done apologizing, he took her to the gym and that's where Chancey's training began.

Seven years after the first time he brought her to that gym, the place where he taught her everything she knew about life's mental and physical challenges, the place where she trained and learned how to fight for her life, it was the same place her father took his last breath. They murdered her father in the backroom of the gym while she was in the ring training, learning how to fight, learning how survive, learning how not to back down. She was in the ring fighting, and her father was on the floor dying. He was dying in the same building where he taught her all the important lessons she'd need to know to make it through life.

Both plates of food had been pushed toward the center of the table. The once succulent ribs and rich creamed spinach now looked cold and sad, much like how Chancey and Otis felt.

The two of them sat there slouched down in their seats looking defeated. In the still and deafening silence, they took turns staring at one another, both of them looking straight ahead without actually seeing the other person in front of them. They only saw the problems ahead and the good days behind them. They had been here before. Otis's kitchen held so many secrets it could rival that of any Catholic confessional. It was several years ago when they sat at that table and Chancey told Otis about the night her father died. The mood in the kitchen that day was a lot like the moment they were currently in. It was all too familiar and way too uncomfortable. They'd been here before, but they were older now, and things were not the same.

As he looked at Chancey, Otis could only see the child that she used to be. The one who said the exact same words to him over a decade ago, words she had actually believed back then when she said them for the first time. But she was older now, and he knew that she knew better now. Everything would not be okay, and Otis in good conscience could make no promises for her safety, not this time around. This time around, in his opinion, to offer her or anyone false hope was the worst thing you could do to a person. So, instead of hoping and fantasizing, Otis prayed. He silently prayed to God for her safety, he prayed every prayer he could think of and called on any grace that might have been set aside for him to be quickly transferred over to her. Chancey had always been in Otis's prayer, but after that night, she is where *all* of his prayers went—every single one of them.

***

"Hey you."

Startled, Otis dropped the tomato he'd been rubbing with his thumb, searching for signs of bruising. He grunted as he watched it tumble back down into the bin from where it came. "Damnit, Chancey! What you sneaking up me like that for? Now I got to sit here and sift through these damn tomatoes all over again to find the right ones."

Slightly amused by how upset he was, Chancey couldn't help but chuckle in response.

"And ain't shit funny either." Shaking his head as he sighed and looked back down at the bin of tomatoes, Otis reluctantly reached his hand down into the bin to start his selection process one more time. "What you doing over here anyway?"

After settling for the first tomato that looked good to him but was still not as good looking as the one he previously had, Otis shrugged and grunted to himself while he tied a knot in the produce bag. With the tomatoes now secure, it was time to move on. They walked together from the tiny produce section of the store over to the equally small refrigerated section where the meat was. In spite of the limited selection in almost every department, the corner grocery store where Otis shopped had been more of a convenience to him than any large chain grocery in the city. Chancey had been able to persuade him to try one of the larger stores once in the past, but after five minutes inside, he threw his hands up in disgust and stormed out. The corner store was a comfort to him. It had everything he needed and the people there knew who he was; they were consistent and honest about their products, and that meant more than variety and discount to him.

"How you know where I was anyway?"

Smiling, she handed him a pack of steaks with a bright orange sticker attached. "'Cause it's Tuesday."

"And?"

Taping the corner of the pack in his hand, Chancey shook her head. "Tuesday is *Manager's Special* day on the meats."

Letting out a low grumble while gazing at the steaks he'd been handed, Otis knew he couldn't argue with the truth. "You think you're so damn smart."

"What you cooking tonight? I was thinking I might pass through."

Otis sucked his teeth as he scowled at Chancey and mumbled to himself.

"Well, what's that all about?"

Turning up his nose in response to the question, Otis kept his head down and his mouth shut.

"Mr. Otis?"

Confused, Chancey turned and leaned against the meat case so she could face Otis, then with both hands she reached out and softly clasped her hand around his wrist. "Mr. Otis, what's wrong?"

Sighing as he lifted his head and turned his attention away from the meat and set his eyes on Chancey's face, he exhaled deeply and quietly looked at her. "That's all you got planned tonight is my place?"

"Am I not allowed to stop by anymore?" Stunned, Chancey slowly withdrew her hands from Otis' wrist and let her arms fall limply to either side of her.

"Chancey . . ." Otis placed his basket inside the meat bin to free his hands so that he could better search for the words he wanted her to hear. "Chancey, you know you can stop by whenever you want. I just wish you were stopping by on your way to or from something good. You always just passing through shit. You never make plans to do nothing, or see anybody. You never go anywhere."

"That's not true." Defensive, Chancey stood up straight and folded her arms across her chest as she stared back at Otis. "I made plans to go to Louisiana. I made plans. I probably shouldn't have considering how things went, but I did in fact make plans."

"You know that's not what I mean. And Louisiana wasn't so much of a plan as it was a new hiding place. And look what happened. At the first sign of trouble what'd you do? You ran. Ran the same way you always do. You ran right back to the city you ran away from, and now you running all over town trying to hide from your past."

Snatching the basket out the meat bin, Chancey slowly began walking forward. With her eyes fixed on the floor, she kicked her foot at the invisible object in her path as she mumbled to herself. From the corner of her eye, she spotted a pack of pork chops with the big orange sticker that made her stop in her tracks. After picking up the pork chops, she held it over the basket for Otis to look at and approve before she dropped them inside. With the meats all taken care of, they silently turned the corner to the dairy section.

Once they were side by side again, Chancey looked over at Otis and shrugged. "So, you would rather have me stay in Louisiana? With everything I told you that happened, you think I should have stayed down there?"

"That ain't what I said. And you know damn well I don't want you nowhere near any part of that mess. Hold on."

After pausing, Otis gave Chancey a quick pat on the back of the shoulder and pointed at the dairy refrigerator. "Reach in there and get me a container of that half and half for my coffee. I think I'm almost out."

The coffee creamer was Otis's fourth item in his basket. He never purchased more than ten things at a time. Initially, Chancey thought it was because of the weight of the items, that maybe he had a hard time carrying everything home. But that wasn't the reason at all. Chancey quickly learned that Otis could make ten things last two weeks. For him, it wasn't about the weight of things; it was about the waste of things, and Otis didn't waste anything, not his time, his money, or anything else.

She looked down into his basket and could guess the next items on his list. If he was almost out of creamer, then he was also low on coffee, so he'd need a jar of Sanka. Of all the coffees to choose from, he chose the one that came in the smallest jar. Then of course he would need some bread to make sandwiches for the pork chops. Then he would need some eggs to go with his steaks and a bag of potato chips because every main dish needs a side of chips according to Otis, and lastly, a one liter bottle of ginger ale.

As they reached the end of the refrigerated aisle and Chancey handed Otis a carton of eggs, she knew their grocery store date was coming to an end. As they made their way to the checkout, they would pass the last two aisles that contained everything else Otis needed.

"When we get around this corner, go down that aisle and get me—"

"A loaf of bread. Yes, I know."

"Well, if you know so much, what you still doing standing here for? Go on and get the bread."

"I'm going."

As she made her way down the bread aisle, she could hear Otis's feet shuffling to the aisle next to her. After grabbing the bread, she looked up at the ceiling and smiled. "What about coffee?"

"Oh shit, I almost forgot. Yeah, while you over there get me a jar—"

"Of Sanka. Yes, I know."

Laughing at the grumbling she could hear coming from him between the aisles, Chancey grabbed the Sanka and headed to the checkout.

After leaving the corner store, Chancey took the ten-minute walk to Otis's apartment with him. She didn't walk with him to help him carry his groceries; he was more than capable of that. She walked with him to finish the conversation they'd started earlier.

"Just leave the bags on the table. I'll get to it in a minute."

"You trying to get rid of me already?" As she placed the bags on the table, she looked over her shoulder at Otis and raised an eyebrow at him.

"Here you go again."

"Me? You started it, Mr. Otis. All I was trying to do was spend some time with you."

She took a seat on the stool he had pushed up against the wall in his kitchen—his *telephone chair* as he called it, because it sat underneath the corded phone that was mounted to the wall, and it was where he could be found siting whenever he got a call at home.

"Chancey, I'm a janitor . . . an ex-con in my late seventies and near the end of my life. Is it gonna take for me to die for you to start to live?"

Before she could answer, she looked at Otis whose hand was raised silently halting her from speaking. "Now, your father, your mother, and even your brother, maybe they didn't do too much with their lives by other people's standards, but they did what they could in the time that they had. But you, you ain't done nothing, Chance. Surviving ain't living. You keep surviving to die another day. You better learn how to live so you have something to survive for. In spite of everything you've been through, you're still here. You ain't dead, you ain't crazy, and that's a blessing. Go do something with your life, do something that they never got the chance to do with theirs. Look now, they may have lost the fight, but they all went down swinging, all of them. Your father taught you to never back down. You gotta fight for the life you want."

CHAPTER FOURTEEN

Almost two weeks had gone by since Chancey had last seen Otis, which was highly unusual for her, but what was more unusual was that she was angry with him. She was angry with him for judging her and for daring her to create a life that she knew better than to hope to have; after all, he was the one who had always warned her that *hope* is the most dangerous of all drugs. The way she saw it, hope had killed her father, her mother, and her brother. Of all the dangers seen and unseen, hope was what frightened her the most.

Despite still being mad at him for what he said, she couldn't stay away any longer than she had. Otis was her whole heart, and no matter what he did or said, her heart just didn't beat right without him.

"Mr. Otis? Hello?"

As she entered the apartment, the sound of Sam Cooke and the smell of Clorox hit her in the face. His Saturdays were just as routine as his Tuesdays. Instead of searching through refrigerated cases of meat for the Manager's Special stickers, on Saturdays the floor was mopped, the walls were wiped down, and the record player would turn and fill the air with the sounds of better days gone by.

"Hey, Chance. Come on in the kitchen. I'm almost through with these walls in here. When I'm done, I'll make us some lunch. You want a sandwich?"

Laughing to herself as she made her way into the kitchen, Chancey shook her head at the comfort of knowing exactly what was going to happen before it did.

"What? What's so funny?" On his way to wipe down the cabinets on the other side of the room, with rag in hand, Otis stopped and looked at Chancey and frowned as he let out a gruff giggle.

"Nothing."

"Well, what you laughing at then?"

"You, Mr. Otis. I'm laughing at you." She plopped down on his *telephone stool*, now laughing out loud. Chancey looked around the kitchen and shrugged. "Mr. Otis, every Saturday you spend the whole morning cleaning your apartment, you spend hours every weekend doing the same thing over and over, cleaning a place that never has a chance to get dirty."

"And that's why it ain't never been dirty, 'cause I give it a good cleaning once every week."

"Now Mr. Otis, you know that's not even the truth. It ain't dirty 'cause you don't even let a crumb hit the floor before you're off getting a rag, mop, or broom to clean it up. And that's you *every* day of the week."

"Oh, hush up, Chancey. You always over here minding my damn business." No matter how accurate her comments were, they still didn't stop Otis from walking over to the sink and wiping down the cabinets. "What you want for lunch today? I got some liverwurst in there. I can make us some sandwiches."

"Ew, no. You know I don't eat liverwurst. And anyway, I came over to take you out to lunch today."

With his back facing her and his arm still extended toward the cabinet mid-wipe down, Otis paused and glanced over his shoulder.

"Just 'cause?"

"*Just 'cause,* huh?" Satisfied with the work he had done, Otis took the rag and draped it over the faucet before shuffling his way over the kitchen table to sit down and rest. "No, I don't think I wanna go out and eat today. I've been in here cleaning all morning. I just want to sit and relax. I ain't trying to change my clothes and do a whole bunch of shit just to eat lunch."

"Who said you had to change? I only wanted to go to the chicken spot two blocks down."

"Oh—the chicken joint? They open today?"

"Yeah, they open. Come on, Mr. Otis, come get out the house and get some fresh air with me. Let's go eat some chicken and then you can come home to your nice clean apartment and put your feet up and relax."

As he shuffled his feet back and forth under the table, Otis tapped his finger on the windowsill and sighed. "I really ain't feel like leaving the house today, but that chicken *is* good. Them girls down there know how to fry the hell out some chicken."

Smiling from ear to ear, Chancey nodded in agreement. "Okay, let's go then."

After agreeing to walk the two blocks to the chicken spot—the chicken spot that according to the both of them made the *best chicken in DC*—halfway into their walk, Otis stopped in the middle of the sidewalk. "Girl, I forgot to tell you what happened to me the other day."

Stunned and concerned, Chancey closed the one-foot gap between them as she searched Otis's face for signs of distress. She was always afraid something might happen to him. His age and slow movement did little to deter him from doing most anything he wanted to do, but his determination and fearlessness scared the hell out of Chancey. She was always worried about his health and well-being. When he stopped in the middle of the sidewalk, her heart stopped as well.

"What, Mr. Otis? You okay? You need to sit down?"

"No, I don't need to sit down. You're gonna need to sit down when I tell you what happened." Quickly looking both ways to make sure no one was around listening to what he was about to say, Otis leaned in close to Chancey, his eyes making one last look up and down the sidewalk. "My number hit the other day."

"Your—" Annoyed, Chancey leaned back and gave Otis a skeptical side eye. "Mr. Otis, really? You just scared me half to death. Got me thinking you're having a heart attack right here in the middle of the street . . . and just to tell me your numbers hit. Really, Mr. Otis?"

"What you mean *just*? I been playing them same damn numbers for years. Every week on Friday night on my way home, I stop and get me a Pepsi, a Mr. Goodbar, and I play my numbers before I go in the house. Every week the same thing, and every week when them numbers come out— nothing. But this week . . . this week, I hit them numbers straight!"

Not only did Chaney not gamble with her life, but she didn't gamble with her money either. The lottery never made sense to her. To Chancey, the lottery was nothing but a creative but legal way to sell people the most dangerous drug of all: hope.

"Okay, so how much did you win?"

Moving closer to fill the space she'd created when she realized there was no crisis in health, Otis once again looked around to ensure no one was listening. "Two hundred and fifty thousand dollars."

"Two hundred—"

"Shh. Hush. Why you so damn loud?"

Quickly covering her mouth with her hand, she now, too, found herself searching the area for listening ears. Chancey opened her eyes wide and stared at Otis in disbelief. "Are you serious, Mr. Otis?"

"Come on, keep walking." As he turned to continue walking down the sidewalk, Otis chuckled to himself. "I knew them numbers were gonna come out eventually."

"What you gonna do with the money?"

Shrugging his shoulders as they reached the end of the block and turned the corner, Otis licked his lips in anticipation of the meal that he could now smell. "Well, I'm gonna put some in the bank, and I think I just might go out and get me a new recliner."

"A new recliner? That's all?"

"Well, I don't need nothing else right now."

"Mr. Otis, you been playing them same numbers for over a decade and you ain't never thought about what you would do if you won? You don't wanna retire or go on a long vacation or nothing?"

"No."

Outside the chicken spot, a couple with their toddler got up from one of the few picnic tables that were outside. Faster then he'd moved all day, Otis shuffled over to the table to claim it. The remnants of the previous family's meal were still on the top the table, but he didn't care. "We got here right on time. You can't never get a seat out here; that's how you know the food is good."

Otis began to push the leftover garbage to one side of the table and sweep away the crumbs. He waived his left hand at Chancey, shooing her away. "You go on in there and get the food; I'll stay out here and watch the table."

"Okay, moneybags, I'm not sure why I should be paying for the food though, you know, considering—"

"Oh, shut the hell up and go get the food."

Shaking his head as he listened to Chancey laughing while she walked off, Otis went back to cleaning the picnic table. He didn't dare get up to throw anything away. Instead, he put all the empty containers and cups in a pile and pushed them as close to the edge of the table as he could without them actually falling off, and then with one of the few clean napkins that was left behind, he gave the table a quick wipe down.

Before he could settle in and wait for Chancey to return, no sooner than he had reached his arm back from placing the napkin with the rest of the garbage pile at the end of the table, there was a large body lowering itself into the seat across from him.

"Hey, what the hell you doing? You don't see me sitting here?"

"You're Otis, right? Otis Benjamin?"

Annoyed and offended, Otis rocked side to side. No one he knew, and no one who truly knew him would ever be so rude and arrogant as to just walk up to his table uninvited and unannounced. "I said, I'm sitting here."

"But you are Otis Benjamin, right?"

Otis turned his head and scowled down the street. Before he could turn back around, he could hear the tapping of fingertips on the table.

He chuckled a little bit as he cleared shis throat before extending his arm across the table toward Otis. "My apologies, Mr. Benjamin, I completely forgot my manners. I was just so thrown off seeing you here, please forgive me. I'm Detective Lorenzo Ducet. We spoke on the phone once before."

With his head still turned away from Lorenzo and his arms now folded defiantly across his chest, Otis cut his eyes in Lorenzo's direction. "You a long way from home, ain't you?"

"I am indeed." Lorenzo smiled and chuckled to himself as he let his arm fall slowly on the table. Clearly he would not be getting a handshake today; he'd be lucky if he got any eye contact at all.

"Yeah, I still haven't been able to get in contact with Ms. Morris by phone, and my investigation is still ongoing."

While he wasn't under arrest, Otis knew his rights and decided he would exercise them by remaining silent.

"Mr. Benjamin, I would really appreciate your cooperation on this. Our city lost a lot of innocent souls, and my department lost a good officer, a caring friend, and loving mother."

With his hands clasped together, leaning forward on the table, Lorenzo tilted his head sideways in an effort to draw Otis's gaze toward him. "Now, from what I've learned about Ms. Chancey Morris, you two are like family. You're the closest thing she has to a father."

Not that he was going to respond to Lorenzo, but before he even had the chance, Israel arrived.

"Detective Saint James, look who I ran into here. Mr. Otis Washington himself. It's a good thing you wanted to stop and get some chicken for lunch today, partner."

As Lorenzo turned to grab some of food from out of Israel's hands that he had just purchased, Israel carefully lifted his leg over the bench to take a seat as he stared down at Otis. Otis could feel Israel's eyes on him, but instead of returning the stare, he looked past Israel and stared behind him at the front door to the restaurant where he could see Chancey, and he could see that she was just about to start approaching the table. As quickly and as discreetly as he could, he made eye contact with her and quickly jerked his head to the side, ushering her to leave . . . and so she did.

Once seated, Israel quickly extended his hand toward Otis. "Hello, Mr. Washington, I'm Detective Israel Saint James." Israel's good intentions were met with the same silence and disregard that had been offered to Lorenzo.

"Yeah, Israel. Mr. Benjamin don't seem too happy to be meeting us. Now why do you think that is, partner?"

"Well, partner, in my experience, people with a lot to say are usually the most difficult ones to get to talk." Israel stuck his straw in his soda and studied Otis. He tried to find signs of tension or anxiety in his body. Israel searched and searched but Otis gave nothing away.

"Mr. Benjamin, it's obvious that you're not happy that we're here. We didn't come all the way up here to upset you, but we do have a job to do. Just tell us where she is." Deciding to give him a moment to think over what had been said, Lorenzo grabbed a chicken wing from the box between him and Israel and took a bite . As he opened his mouth to cool off the meat that was now burning his tongue, steam came out in a small burst, which made him look ridiculous, which annoyed him but amused Otis. Through the pain and the steam, he caught a glimpse of Otis's brief sly grin.

"We just want to talk to her, Mr. Benjamin, that's all." Pushing his plate aside, Israel leaned forward toward Otis. "When we were looking for Chancey we couldn't find her. Every direction we looked for her led us right back to you. You're her home; you're her safe place. We know you know where she is. We're not trying to get her into any trouble. We just want her help."

Deciding enough time had passed, and that Chancey should be long gone from the area, Otis put his palm on the top of the table and pushed himself to his feet.

Confused, Lorenzo pulled his face back from chicken wing that was in front of him and set it back down on the plate. "Hey now, where you going? We just got here. You ain't even gonna get yourself something to eat?" As he reached for a napkin with one hand, he nudged the box of chicken Israel had brought over with the other.

"No. I already ate." Otis nodded his head at the empty containers at the edge of the table before turning and walking away. "I've got errands to run. You two have a safe trip back to New Orleans."

"We're not leaving yet." Lorenzo picked his chicken wing back up and held it in front of his face. "We'll be here a few more days. We're booked at the Verizon Center. Tell your girl to come and talk to us, please. We're not trying to put her in danger, and we know that you're just trying to protect her, but whether you help us or not, we *will* speak with her."

Hearing every word Lorenzo had said, Otis unflinchingly walked off slowly and quietly down the sidewalk in the opposite direction of his home. He was confident Chancey was long gone, but still, he'd rather walk ten blocks in the wrong direction just to be absolutely sure. They knew who he was, and more than likely they knew where he lived, so he knew he couldn't give Chancey shelter. But what he could give her was time—time to get away—and if that meant him walking until his last breath, that is what he was prepared to do.

CHAPTER FIFTEEN

It had been three days since her failed lunch date with Otis—no calls, no unannounced visits, no contact at all. She knew she would eventually have to come out and check to see if the coast was clear, and in truth, she was more concerned about Otis's well-being than her own, and so Chancey decided that today was the day.

Leaning against a lamppost at the end of the street a few blocks away from Otis's apartment, Chancey anxiously searched the area surrounding her for anything and anyone out of the ordinary, trying to remain as nonchalant as she could while she impatiently waited to catch sight of Otis. She'd gotten to the corner a whole hour before his usual shopping time so she would be able to see him walking toward her.

By six thirty that evening, worry began to set in. It was well after the time she expected to have seen Otis. Anxiously shifting her weight from foot to foot as she gnawed on her bottom lip and frantically played invisible piano keys at the sides of her thighs, before her mind had a chance to fully spiral, she could see him in the distance.

Barely managing to hold herself back from lunging straight at him and wrapping her arms around his neck, Chancey bounced up and down in her little section of dimly lit sidewalk. When he was close enough, she reached out with both arms, pulled herself close to him, and let her cheek rest against his.

"Girl, if you don't calm yourself down, jumping up and down like you don't have no damn sense." In the midst of fussing at her, Otis held her tightly as relief washed over him. "All right now, that's enough. Since you're here you might as well come on and shop with me. Come on, let's get in this store before it gets too late."

Inside the corner store, basket in one hand and joy in place of where anxiety had once been, Chancey leaned her head to the side as she studied Otis, who was studying the tomatoes. "Mr. Otis, where have you been? You should have been here over thirty minutes ago. You trying to give me a heart attack?"

"I don't know who you think you talkin' to, little girl. I don't answer to you. And get your hand off your damn hip when you talking to me."

There was a certain level of comfort she found in his response that eased away the rest of the tension she'd been holding in her spine. She smiled back at him as she let her arm drop to her side. "You're usually here earlier than this. Everything okay at the center?"

"Yeah, everything's fine at the center." After rolling three beefsteak tomatoes around in the bin several times, he carefully picked them up, placed them in a plastic bag, and tied it with a slip knot before handing it to Chancey. "Come on this way; I need me a red onion."

With a sudden seriousness in his step, once in front of the onions, with his left hand Otis reached out to grab one but instead his fingertips brushed several of them, causing a few to tumble out of place. Annoyed, Otis let out a tired sigh as he pulled back his arm and looked down at his feet and shook his head. "I was waiting on you."

"Waiting on me?"

"Yeah. I knew you would pop up somewhere. I figured it would be the center, so I stuck around after closing just to see if you'd show up. Did the same thing last night too."

"So, those cops from New Orleans are gone then?"

"Yeah, they should be on their way back home, if they ain't there already."

"Well, what did they say?"

Snatching an onion without his usual examination, Otis sucked his teeth as he shoved it in Chancey's unprepared hands. "They ain't say much, just that they need to speak with you about the shooting."

Quickly shuffling away from the onions but with no clear direction, Otis shook his head and grunted as he turned down the canned vegetable aisle. "I don't like it, Chancey. I don't like it, I don't like it, I don't like it. Not one bit."

Still fumbling trying to open the thin plastic produce bag to put the red onion in, Chancey took turns looking down at the bag and up at Otis, equally confused by both. "Don't like what?"

"I don't like them coming all the way up here looking for you."

"I don't like it either, Mr. Otis, but—"

"But nothing, Chancey. You know too damn much." Stepping in the middle of the aisle, Otis looked around confused before letting out a sigh of exhaustion. "See now, you got me all turned around. I don't need shit from over here. You got my nerves bad. I'm too old for this shit."

When Chancey's father was murdered, Otis had been able to stay on top of things. Any rumors concerning what Chancey *might have known* were quickly quashed, any inclination that the responsible parties might have had to permanently silence the *witness*, who hadn't said a word, Otis made sure all those thoughts were quickly abandoned. He wasn't a young man back then. He was older than most involved, but he wasn't old; now he was old, and all the young men had gotten older. Back then, the threat of the kind of retribution he could rain down was enough to keep Chancey and her brother safe. But he was an old man now, and while people still respected him, they didn't fear him in the same way they once did; they didn't worry about what an old man might do.

It hurt her heart to see Otis so worried about her. She slid closer to him, looped her arms around his, and rested her head on his shoulder. Once she felt him take a few deep breaths, she lifted her head and turned her face toward the side of his cheek as she let her chin rest on the top of his shoulder. She smiled and gave him a kiss on the line where his beard met his skin.

"Mr. Otis, you need to rest. You go home and I'll finish your shopping for you."

After reaching his arm over to softly pat the side of her head, Otis headed for the door. Once he'd made it there, he laid his palm against the glass of the door and stood there silently for a few moments before he gave the door a push. When the door was slightly cracked, he flinched as a burst of air hit his face and he quickly turned back and looked at Chancey. The mere sight of her warmed his heart. She was his everything, and no matter what she did or didn't do in life, he was proud of her. He was always proud of her. Otis smiled to himself as he watched her look around the store trying to decide which aisle to head to next. "Don't forget my chopped meat. When you get in I'ma fix us some burgers tonight."

"I was just heading that way to get it."

"Oh, hush now, stop that lying. You ain't know I was making burgers 'til just now when I told you."

"The red onion and tomatoes, Mr. Otis. What's a burger without some sautéed red onions and thick juicy tomatoes."

Smiling as he gave her a quick swat with his hand, Otis pushed open the door and looked up at the sky before glancing back at Chancey one last time and laughing as he shook his head.

Twenty minutes after Otis had left her in the store, Chancey had finally made it to the front of the checkout line. Shopping at this time of night meant the line was longer than usual. The store was full of people getting their last-minute items for their meals. If they had arrived at Otis's normal shopping time, she would have already been checked out and probably walking in the apartment side by side with him. Nevertheless, she was done and finally on her way to his apartment.

She climbed the few steps to get into Otis's building and laughed to herself because she knew no matter how tired he seemed or how old he claimed to be, the man would not be sitting down resting when she got in. She knew he would be standing in the kitchen waiting on her to bring him the chopped meat so he could cook her some dinner.

Once inside the apartment, Chancey's breath was immediately swept away. What she expected to see when she walked in and what she was actually seeing were two completely different things. Otis wasn't in the kitchen waiting for her. He also wasn't resting in his recliner with his feet up; what he was doing was lying silently on the floor in his living room—bleeding. Unable to hold the blood back, as it appeared he'd been trying to do, his hands now lay limply by his stomach covered in his blood that would not stop flowing.

With her mouth hanging open in shock, Chancey dropped the grocery bags in her hand, but before she could take a breath, before she could even say his name, she was on her knees by his side frantically trying to use her hands to close the wound and make the bleeding stop.

"Otis, Mr. Otis, wake up please. Please, Mr. Otis. Mr. Otis, please wake up." The tears rushed down her cheeks, and Chancey gasped for breath as she reached down and touched the side of Otis's face with her hand, leaving traces of bright red blood on his salt-and-pepper beard. "No, no, no. Mr. Otis, please. Please don't go, Mr. Otis, please."

In her heart of hearts, she knew her pleading was in vain. She'd been here before, this place of desperation, and she already knew the end result. And yet, despite everything she knew, she couldn't help herself from *hoping*, that this time it would be different. She stared down at Otis, praying he would open his eyes, praying that he would take a breath, but neither of those things happened. Otis couldn't open his eyes. Otis couldn't see her. Otis couldn't see anything. His eyes were closed and not even an eyelash fluttered.

As her mind conceded to the fact that no matter how hard she cried, Otis's eyes were not going to open, she stopped her pleading and laid her chin on his chest. But before she could even think to question *why*, on the other side of Otis, standing in a pool of the old man's blood stood Detective Israel Saint James .

CHAPTER SIXTEEN

"You need to put pressure on that wound!"

Israel was on his knees and halfway out of his long flannel shirt before Chancey could even recognize who he was. Israel quickly wound up as much of his shirt as he could around his right hand and pressed down firmly on the wound, which was now seeping blood instead of gushing it. With his left hand he reached for Otis's neck and tried to feel for a pulse.

"What happened here?" After feeling for a pulse in Otis and finding none, and waiting for a response from Chancey and receiving none, Israel took out his phone and called 911. "God damnit! Mr. Benjamin, don't do this, sir. Come on back." Shaking his head in disgust, Israel looked down at Otis and felt defeated. "Hello? I need paramedics dispatched please to the seventeen hundred block of Florida Avenue in North East."

Outside of the sound of Israel's voice, the room was silent and still. Chancey was still kneeling on the opposite side of Otis, her arms limp at her sides, her blood-covered palms lay lifelessly on the floor pointed at the ceiling, and her eyes that looked straight ahead but saw nothing continued to release tear after tear after tear.

For a moment, Israel shifted his attention from Otis to Chancey. The pain she felt in that moment was far greater than anything Otis was currently feeling, and the brief sight of her heartache made him wince and shutter before he quickly turned his attention back to the old man, who in truth, he knew felt nothing at all. "Yes, operator, I'm still here. It's an elderly male. Late seventies, stab wound to the abdomen . . . no pulse."

After ending the call with the 911 operator, Israel straightened up but remained kneeling by Otis's side across from Chancey. His bloody hands that were once resting on Otis were now resting on his thighs. Israel looked deeply into Chancey's eyes and searched for her.

"I know there isn't a thing I could say to you right now, Ms. Morris, to comfort you, but from the bottom of my heart, you have my most sincere condolences. Mr. Benjamin seemed like a good man, a hardworking, good man, and I know he loved you something fierce. From my heart to yours . . . you have my deepest sympathy." With his left hand over his heart and his head tilted ever so slightly to the floor, and his somber eyes fixed on Chancey, Israel shook his head slowly in dismay. "I am so very sorry for your loss."

It was less than five minutes since he'd hung up with 911, and DC Metro was already at the door. Chancey sat silently by Otis's side. Her eyes were nearly swollen shut from the tears that just wouldn't stop falling. The exchanges between Israel and DC Metro, DC Metro amongst themselves, and the radio operators all sounded like buzzing in her ear. The light in the hallway poured into the dimly lit apartment illuminating the living room where Otis lay feeling nothing and where Chancey knelt in pain. The light came in, and the hurt grew brighter. Otis was the one who had been stabbed, but it was Chancey who felt the pain of the wound, and that pain was excruciating.

Chancey looked down at the man who had cared for her when he didn't have to, loved her when she didn't love herself, the man who had stood beside her and behind her without question or hesitation. She gazed down at his closed eyes, took his hand into hers, and took a deep breath.

"He didn't deserve this."

Everyone in the room stopped talking, and all eyes were on her. Chancey's gaze, which was once on Otis, had now turned to a glare and was fixed on Israel. "He didn't deserve this. He didn't deserve this. *He didn't deserve this!*"

Israel locked eyes with Chancey as he slowly made his way back over to Otis's lifeless body, and with his eyes fixed on hers, he squatted down next to her and clasped his bloodstained hands in front of him. He exhaled slowly. "No, my darling, no he did not . . . he did not deserve this."

It took almost an hour for the coroner to get to Otis's apartment and take his body. It would have taken longer than that had the lead detective there not called in a favor to get them there sooner. Chancey refused to leave Otis's side. They needed her to leave, to go to the precinct where they could take her statement, but Chancey would not be moved. She held his hand in hers until they placed his body on the stretcher. Her last tear fell once they pulled the white sheet over his head. She followed the stretcher and watched the men load Otis's body into the back of their van, and she stood silently in the street until they drove away and were out of sight.

Once Otis was gone, in body and in spirit, Chancey left the apartment willingly with DC Metro so that she could go and give her statement. Her time spent there in their interview room was brief. They looked her up before they began the interview, but most had already known who she was and the circumstances that she had come from, and they were all pretty confident she had nothing to do with the death of Otis Benjamin. But still they had to ask some routine questions: *Who was Otis Benjamin to her?* For Chancey, that question required no thought, and her answer came with zero hesitation. "Mr. Otis was my everything." And of course they needed to know, *Why was she visiting him that evening?* It was silly and simple, but it was also the truth: *burgers.* "We were gonna talk and watch *Good Times* and eat some burgers." And last but not least, *Did she know anyone who would have wanted to harm Otis Benjamin?* That question struck a spark behind her eyes because of course not, "Hurt him? No one wanted to hurt Mr. Otis. Not him…"

Based on her statement, the detectives could go back and retrace Chancey's and Otis's steps from earlier that evening. The neighborhood they shopped in had cameras all over, so if they really needed to verify her alibi, they could, but they knew it wouldn't be necessary. They never asked her, and she never had to say that she didn't kill Mr. Otis. They could see it in her eyes, they heard it in her voice, and the movement of her chest as she tried to remember to breathe. And what they couldn't see in her there in that room, they saw in her past from her file, from the rumors and the gossip of the circumstances of her life. They pitied her. There was a sadness that haunted her that could be felt in her presence. They didn't ask her if she killed him; she never said that she did, but she did feel responsible. And as she sat there, the guilt and the sorrow in her chest slowly began to fester and turn into rage.

Once she was done and on her way out of the precinct, she found herself suddenly dazed by the world. She stepped out of the precinct door and stepped into a world without Otis. The weight of knowing he wasn't out there, he wasn't anywhere anymore, it hit her heart and her head at the same time and the sensation left her dazed and breathless.

"You all right, Ms. Morris?"

Leaning down toward Chancey, who was doubled over and on the verge of hyperventilating, her hand pressed against the glass on the door of the precinct and her head faced downward toward the pavement as she tried to catch her breath. Israel extended his arm for support as he waited for her to calm herself.

Out of instinct, one she didn't know she had, Chancey seized Israel's arm and held on to it tightly.

"Just breathe, Chancey. Slow breaths." With his free hand, Israel slowly rubbed the space between her shoulder and tried his best to keep her calm. It was there on the precinct steps that Israel, the man who threatened to bring a catastrophic storm into her life with unspeakable consequences, suddenly became her anchor. "Just keep breathing."

Eventually, once she could feel the ground beneath her feet again, she stood up straight. With her hand still clasped around Israel's forearm, she turned to face him and took a deep breath. Her eyes and her throat both filled with tears, and she reached out her other hand to him, placing it on his chest. "I have nothing to live for now. He was all I had."

CHAPTER SEVENTEEN

"You got a look in your eyes I ain't never think I'd see again."

Israel shifted his gaze from the nothingness he'd been staring into in front of him and looked back down at the half-drunk glass of bourbon in his hand. "I got a look, huh? And you say it's one you've seen before, Ms. Shirlene? I don't know about that. I don't know if you ever seen *this* particular look before."

"Oh, I've seen it. It was a long time ago, but I've seen it. You don't forget a look like that. It's cold and hollow—dark enough to stop a beating heart." Shirlene sighed as she leaned across the top of the bar and let her head hang as she shook it. "Looks like this Quarter is one man short compassion tonight."

"You saying, I ain't got no compassion in me, Ms. Shirlene?"

"None that I can see from where I stand, Israel."

"Now, that's a damn shame, Ms. Shirlene. I don't think this Quarter can afford to lose any compassion. After everything it's been through, everything it's still going through." Israel exhaled deeply as he sat up straight and looked down into his glass before gulping down the remainder of the dark liquor inside. "Once a man's compassion is gone, then all hope is lost and there's no coming back from that."

"Ain't that the truth." Unafraid and unmoved by the look that she was all too familiar with, Shirlene grabbed a glass from the shelf and poured herself a glass of bourbon after topping off Israel's. Once full, she softly clanked the brim of her glass against his and nodded. "Sante."

Elbows on the bar top and fingers circling the brim of the now empty glass in front of her, Shirlene looked intently at Israel and studied his anguished face. "So, you gonna tell me what's got you troubled?"

"I met a girl."

"You always meeting girls, Israel. What's different about this one?"

"This girl's very different. She reminds me of this young boy I used to know—this boy with this cold, hollow look in his eyes. You know the one I'm talking 'bout?"

"Yeah, I know the one."

Taking his hand and rubbing it against the rough stubble on his unshaven face, Israel inhaled deeply and shut his eyes. As he slowly exhaled, his eyelids lifted and his eyes found Shirlene's. He silently searched her chestnut-colored eyes for the memory of the boy's face that they spoke of.

"So, this girl you met reminds you of this boy you used to know, and that's what's got you troubled?"

"No, Ms. Shirlene, no it's not that she reminds me of him that's got me troubled."

"Then what is it, Israel?"

"This girl—this girl, Shirlene, she told me a story you wouldn't believe."

Never before had it taken Shirlene this long to get to the heart of the matter with Israel. They weren't blood, but they were family; they were closer to one another that any blood relatives they knew. The look in Israel's eyes, and the not knowing what was going on in his mind, was making her anxious and uncomfortable. Shirlene quickly snatched the bourbon bottle and with it took back control of her nerves as she poured them both another glass. "Told you a story, did she? A story about what?"

"Not *what*." Israel slowly shook his head as he lifted the glass to his mouth and took a gulp. "*Who*. It is *who* the story is about and who's in it that's brought me to this place." As he sighed, his exhaustion echoed in the air and blared against the silence that was once between them, and as if he could visually see the disturbance, as if the soundwaves were dancing in technicolor in front of him, Israel frowned before slowly shaking his head in despair.

"Now, I would never have guessed it, Ms. Shirlene, and you probably could've knocked me down with a feather after she told me, that's how shocked I was." As he paused to take another gulp from his glass, Israel looked over at Shirlene and bit his bottom lip in frustration. The bags underneath his eyes carried so much more than tiredness from lack of sleep; they carried weariness, they carried a weight that he couldn't hold in his hands because it was too heavy.

"You was in that story too, Ms. Shirlene. The story this girl told me, Shirlene . . . you was in that story."

"I was in the story?"

"You was in the story, Ms. Shirlene."

"The hell you say."

"I say, Ms. Shirlene; I say."

Shirlene stood up straight and took a quick look around the bar. Aside from her and Israel, there was only three other people in the bar, but it was three too many for her. "It's closing time!"

With her hands on her hips, Shirlene stared at each patron individually, her eyes daring them not to comply; none of them were that stupid, of course. "Leave the money on the table and get on out. Get home safe."

Walls couldn't talk, but people could . . . and did. Once the last person stumbled out the door and Shirlene could hear it click shut, she put one determined foot in front of the other and walked from behind the bar and took a seat beside Israel. As she reached across the bar top for the bourbon bottle, she raised an eyebrow at him and then slowly topped off both their glasses. "Now, this story . . . sounds like it's one I need to hear."

Still facing forward, Israel tilted his head toward Shirlene and nodded. "Yes, ma'am, it is. That it is."

"Well, go on then. I need to hear who dun put *me* in a story. Thought folks 'round here had better sense than that."

Israel smiled as he let out a small huff and fingered the rim of his glass. "That right there is why I love you, that and a few other things that we won't get in to. Also, I love you, Shirlene, because you've never lied to me. In all the years that I've known you, you've never lied to me and you've always had my back."

Israel took his glass and tapped it against Shirlene's. "Sante."

Shirlene quickly grabbed her glass off the bar and raised it to Israel. "Sante."

Israel turned his body to face Shirlene and put his hand up to his heart. "You're the reason I can walk these streets. It's not the gun or the badge, it's you. And I thank you for that, Shirlene. From the bottom of my heart, I thank you."

Reaching out to him and covering his hand with her own. Shirlene gave Israel's hand a gentle pat and a firm squeeze. "That's right, you know you won't ever walk alone, baby. Not while there's still breath in this old body."

Nodding in understanding as he exhaled, Israel rubbed his chest in appreciation. "The girl, the witness that me and Lorenzo was looking for—well, we went up to Washington, DC, and we found her. We found Ms. Chancey Morris. We found her, and Ms. Shirlene, she told me a story. Now, I knew she heard something that day. Turns out, Ms. Shirlene, she heard *everything*."

"So, she told you who shot up the store and killed Victoria?"

"Yeah, she told me. And it wasn't the shooter that day who killed her."

"No, baby, no it wasn't."

"Victoria wasn't who I thought she was."

"No, no she wasn't."

So far, Shirlene wasn't surprised or confused by anything that Israel had said. "So, this Chancey, she's a *grave digger* then. She told you a ghost story."

"That she did. But from what she told me, Victoria was the one haunting people with her lies, and she was doing it long before she was put in her grave."

"Yes, she was."

"Decent people. Not the best of folks, but decent people."

Shirlene shut her eyes and nodded in agreement. Just like the people he spoke of, she also considered herself a decent person. She wasn't the best of folks by societies standards, but she was decent, and she was the best person she knew how to be. Shirlene stayed true to herself and the people she cared about no matter the cost to her. "What else did she tell you, Israel?"

"Everything. She told me everything. I know why Baby Ruth Anne came running to you that night. I know Victoria played a big hand in her own death. And I know, I know—" Israel shut his eyes and clasped his hands together and let them rest on his lap. "I know to make this right, a whole lotta wrong got to be done. We took something from her."

"Took what, from who?"

"Chancey. We took something from her and it ain't right."

"Took what?"

"Her reason for being. The hope in her heart . . . the only thing she had left in this world. We took everything from her, Shirlene."

"Looks like you created a dangerous woman then. I'd have to think long and hard about crossing a woman like that. A woman with nothing to lose is a rare and dangerous breed. Anger like that . . . she could just about set fire to the rain."

After finishing her glass, Shirlene extended her arm out toward Israel, softly grabbed his chin, and held it in the palm of her hand. "She gained something too, Israel. She still has one thing. She may not know it. You might have to show her, but I can see it as clearly as I can see your face in front of me now. She's got you."

"Is that right?"

"Yes. You know it and I know it. Behind that dark stare, I can see she's done sparked a fire in your heart; there's smoke rising behind those dark eyes. I can see it. She ain't lost it all, no sir. She just don't know what she's got, not yet. But she's got more than most, a whole lot more."

"And you say that's me. And considering what we took from her, having me ain't gonna mean much to her now, or to anybody else for that matter."

"Israel, you're another one I'd be reluctant to cross. You are as compassionate as you are courageous and relentless; even if I wasn't who I was to you, I'd still never wrong you, and may God have mercy on the fools that do try and cross you . . . 'cause surely you will not."

Shirlene smiled to herself as she grabbed the bourbon bottle and poured the last of the bottle between their two glasses. "She's got a champion, Israel. She don't know it, but that's exactly what she got. A champion." With her glass in the air, Shirlene nodded and shut her eyes and smiled once she heard Israel's glass clink hers. "Sante."

"Sante."

After sitting her empty glass on the bar, Shirlene got up slowly and shook off a shiver that was creeping up her spine. "Rains coming. I can feel it in my bones."

Israel let his bottom lip roll out slowly from under his front teeth as he shrugged his shoulders in ambivalence. "Let it rain."

CHAPTER EIGHTEEN

"Hey, partner. How you doin' this morning?"

"I'm all right. What's good with you this morning, Lorenzo? Seems like you in a real good mood today."

That Wednesday morning looked the same as all the others, but for Israel it was the first time he walked into the precinct and felt like he didn't belong there.

Lorenzo smiled as he leaned back in his chair and casually shrugged his shoulders. The pen he'd been twirling between his fingers carelessly fell onto his desk as he raised both eyebrows.

"Nothing. I guess I'm just glad to be back home. I hate traveling."

"Yeah. Me too."

"Where'd you get off to yesterday after we landed? I called your phone to see if you wanted to get in a round of hoops with me and some of the fellas, but your phone went straight to voicemail."

As Lorenzo took his seat, he took a quick look around the room that had once felt like a home to him.

"Went down to the Quarter to throw back a few."

"Where? Down to Shirlene's place?"

117

"Yeah. You know I can't step foot in the Quarter and not go by and see my baby Shirlene."

"I tell you, I will never understand . . ."

Before Lorenzo could finish his sentence, he jerked forward in his seat to answer the phone that had begun ringing. "Homicide. This is Detective Lorenzo Ducet." A few nods later, Lorenzo looked over at Israel and threw his hands up as he got to his feet. "Looks like we caught a case, partner. Let's go."

The crime scene they'd been sent to was only six blocks away from the precinct, so the ride to get to it barely took five minutes. As much as Israel didn't want to be around anyone that morning, especially within the confines of a car, he'd have been a fool to try and walk the short distance. Anytime the sun was up in August was a hot day, and today was the hottest it had been that week. Thankfully their presence wasn't required for too long; both the victim and the perpetrator were still at the scene. It was drug deal gone wrong.

"Too bad they can't all be as open and shut as that." As Lorenzo drove the cruiser back to the precinct, he strummed his fingers on the steering wheel as he looked around the busy streets and smiled to himself. "This one shouldn't require too much paperwork either. Once the shooter regains consciousness, we'll go down and get his statement and that's that really. I mean, we already know what happened; the buyer tried to strong-arm the dealer, they both shot at each other, one made it, and one didn't."

"There you have it. Case closed."

Frowning as he looked over at Israel, Lorenzo squinted his eyes as he studied his partner's face.

"All right now, what's going on with you? You been in a mood since we left DC."

Israel sighed as he rubbed his chin and stared out at the street. "Just tired, partner, that's all. Every day it's the same thing; life after life cut short and for what?"

"Israel, we work in homicide. What did you expect?"

"I know. I know we work in homicide, I just always looked at our cases as a way to bring people closure. I used to think that finding the answers helped the ones who lost someone to at least find a little peace in the senselessness of it all."

"And now?'

"And now—and now, I just don't see the point of it all. Seems like I'm always out of reach of peace no matter how many answers I find. My path to peace just keeps leading me to more trouble. I don't know, I'm thinking maybe I might need to take a step back from things."

"A step back? Hold on."

Completely caught off guard, Lorenzo made a sharp right turn and pulled over to the side of the road. "What you mean, *take a step back*? You thinking about transferring to another division?"

"Not transferring. Thinking about stepping away from all of it."

"Turning in your badge? Are you serious? Israel, man, come on, you can't be serious? Talk to me man, what's going on?"

"Nothing's going on, Lorenzo. I'm just tired of it all. Tired of death following me everywhere I go."

Agitated by what he was hearing, Lorenzo took his seat belt off so he could turn and face Israel. "Is this about DC? Israel, brother, there was nothing that you could do. You tried to save him. That man's death is not on you."

"That man did not deserve to die like that. Everywhere I go, Lorenzo, it follows me; even when I'm not looking for it, I see it and I can't stop it. It's wearing me down."

"Then take a break, but don't quit, that ain't you. That don't even sound like you."

After giving Israel a gentle shove on the shoulder, Lorenzo shook his head as he turned back around and put his seat belt back on. "Look, I know what you mean about being tired. I was right there with you not too long ago. Victoria's murder had me questioning everything. I thought about turning my badge in too, but I didn't. I didn't turn it in because I know we make a difference. You and I, Saint James, we're the same; we will not rest until justice is served, and yeah, it can be tiring, but there's people out there depending on us and we cannot let them down. You're a good detective, Israel. New Orleans needs you."

After starting the car again, before he pulled off, Lorenzo gave Israel a few affirming pats on the back. "Now, we got a lead on the corner store shooting, and we'll be able to close that case soon and get justice for Victoria, and then after that, you can step away and take a break. A *break*, Israel, meaning temporary, not permanent. You're not quitting—*Quit*, nah, that ain't in you, brother. You wouldn't even know how to begin to do something like that."

By the time they got back to the precinct, Israel's mood remained unchanged. Lorenzo, seeing this, decided to give him space and proceed with his day sans his partner's normal good-natured humor and fortitude.

Toward the later part of the afternoon, after receiving a call from the hospital that their shooter had regained consciousness, Lorenzo made the trip to the hospital alone to take his statement. It was around the same time Israel had ordered his lunch, so Lorenzo volunteered to go to the hospital alone. He was hoping that a little food and some quiet time might help improve Israel's mood. Additionally, he knew before he left that the hospital visit to get some answers was a fool's errand. He wouldn't get any answers. He'd be lucky if he got a question out before the suspect asked for a lawyer. As senseless as he may have thought it was, it was necessary, it was a formality, it was a procedure required of him for the position he held. He was supposed to *try*. He had to at least make an effort regardless of his personal opinion.

Israel sat at his desk thankful that he didn't have to listen to any more lies that afternoon. He'd have gone to the hospital if he had to, but he was grateful that he wasn't needed, and like Lorenzo, he, too, knew that it was a waste of time. As he sat at his desk waiting for his lunch to be delivered, he decided to run a background check on Chancey. Lorenzo had looked into Chancey previously, which was how he knew she was good at hiding. Unable to get her out of his mind, Israel decided to try and get to know her better, to know more about her and exactly who it was she'd been running from for so very long.

There wasn't much in the system on Chancey, not the adult woman he knew anyway. But adolescent Chancey Morris, that girl had a past, and the path that led her into adulthood had been a long, hard road. Chancey Morris was the only daughter of Mark and Desiree Morris. She had one brother, Roman Morris, who was two years her junior. She grew up in Southeast Washington, DC, in a two-bedroom apartment in a sketchy area. Her father was an ex-con who drove a delivery truck during the day and spent his evenings teaching his daughter how to box. There were also a few news articles about her wins in the local paper. According to the news, Chancey was as good, if not better, than any male boxer her age.

Mark Morris was shot and killed in the back room of the gym where he trained his daughter. Chancey was fourteen years old at the time. The case was unsolved but thought to be drug related. The police had no leads. Their best guess was that the shooters entered the gym through the door off the side alley and surprised her father. Chancey was there that evening, but she was in the ring training; she didn't see a thing. His widow, her mother, Desiree Morris, became a repeat offender after his death. She had numerous drug solicitation charges and eventually she ended up drinking herself to death. No matter how hard she tried, Desiree couldn't find peace after the man she loved had been taken from her. Though she never found peace, she constantly sought it out. She sought it out with fearlessness at first, for the sake of her kids, but the longer she looked the harder it became to find, and then the pain just became more than she could bear. Numbness is what she began to crave and that was an easier find and so she embraced it wholeheartedly until eventually she became still—completely and permanently still—and then that which she sought had finally found her. Peace finally found Desiree. She shut her eyes one sunny Sunday afternoon and never opened them again.

Chancey's brother, Roman Morris, despite their losses, graduated at the top of his class from his high school and received a full academic scholarship to college, a scholarship he never got to use because he, too, was murdered in the streets of DC the summer he graduated. Like his father before him, Roman never received justice; no one was ever held responsible. Roman's case remained unsolved just like his father's.

Israel sighed and slowly released his balled fists as he read the information, rather, lack of information, detailed about Roman's murder. "They took all the fight outta her."

From what he could gather, the only fight Chancey ever lost when she was young wasn't inside the ring she spent nearly every day in; she lost to the world that she was trying to find her place in. She didn't lose to someone bigger or faster, or smarter than she was. She lost to pain and heartache, and she had yet to make a comeback.

Israel's lunch had arrived halfway through his reading, but he was too engrossed with the tragic story that was the life of Chancey Morris to even open the container. Before he knew it, Lorenzo was back.

"That didn't take long."

"Kid shut his eyes as soon as I walked in the room and refused to open them. Opened his mouth for a minute though, just long enough to say the word, *lawyer*."

Lorenzo plopped down in his seat in a huff. "You ain't even eat your lunch. You working on something? Something come in while I was gone?"

"No. No, lunch just got here. They was busy today is all."

Before Lorenzo could inquire any further, his personal cell, which rarely ever rang during the day, started to vibrate.

"Gimme a minute, Saint James. I'ma take this outside."

As he watched Lorenzo walk out, his initial thought was, perhaps he met someone and was starting a relationship. Lorenzo had always been really secretive about his personal life. Even when he and Victoria were dating, the two had been together almost a year before anyone in the department knew.

Any inclination that Israel had about Lorenzo trying to hide the beginning stages of a happy romance were put to rest when Lorenzo came storming back into the room. His fists were clenched, and his jaw was bulging.

"Everything all right, partner?"

Back in his seat, both elbows were propped on the top of his desk and he held his forehead in his palms as he vigorously scratched the top of his head with the tips of his fingers. Lorenzo paused and looked back over at Israel and inhaled deeply. "Uh, just a little disappointing news I just got. It's okay though, I ain't gonna let it get me down."

"Okay. Well, if you need anything you know I'm here."

"Thanks, man."

The change in vibe was palpable. The others in the precinct walked around Israel's and Lorenzo's desks as if they were the gateway to the Bermuda Triangle. The rest of their shift was spent in a shared silence. When the day was over, they were both so distracted by their own personal issues that they parted ways without even saying good night.

CHAPTER NINETEEN

As he pulled into his driveway, Israel sighed, not from exhaustion but from the emotional weight in his chest that he'd been carrying around with him all that day, the weight of knowing that trouble was coming—more accurately, trouble had arrived. It had been there lurking in the darkness and the shadows where he couldn't see it, but now he could see it clearly and he could feel it, and the weight of it was heavy, almost more than he could bear.

His senses had always been good, but now they were on full alert. As he walked up the sidewalk to his home and loosened his tie, he paused before he hit the first step. As he turned his head to look into one of the windows, his eyes squinting in the darkness at what he could not see, he quickly turned up his lip at the darkness and scowled as he leaned forward to take a closer look.

After still not seeing anything but still feeling that something, or someone, was there, he quickly unlocked the front door and gave it a swift kick at the bottom of the frame. Anger began to rise from his abdomen as he leaned against the side of his house and once again tried to lay his eyes on the unknown lurker he knew was there. "I know you're there.

I ain't in the mood for it tonight. So, come on out, or get the hell goin'."

Eyes flickering in the darkness, slowly stepping forward toward Israel, Chancey stuck her hands in her front pockets and then abruptly stopped walking once she was within just a few feet of Israel.

"And where should I go?"

Dumbfounded, Israel took a quick look around the darkness surrounding his home to make sure no one else could see what he was seeing—no eyes peeking through semi-opened blinds, no other shadows lurking in the darkness, and no one on the street taking notice of the meeting. Once he was satisfied that his were the only eyes that could see her, and he was the only one who knew she was there, Israel took a step back and extended one arm toward Chancey, quietly extended the other toward his open door, and invited her in.

"Chancey, I—I . . . how did you—"

Shaking his head in effort to clean out some of the confusion in his mind, Israel inhaled deeply as he took a step forward and closed the gap in between them. "I'm sorry. I didn't mean to sound crazy. I'm just surprised to see you is all. We should probably get from outside and go in and sit down and talk."

With a weak grin and light shrug of the shoulders, Chancey gave a quick nod of agreement and quickly made her way up the steps to Israel's home. As she entered, she looked around and was as surprised as she was impressed. His house was *homey*, but not in an *old man* kind of way. It was inviting, not at all the bachelor pad she thought it would be. The flooring in the home was all hardwood mahogany, no carpets or area rugs anywhere. The floors were simple and classy, and the same could be said about his furniture; it wasn't too big, or small, it was richly colored and had a look of comfort to it. His home was classic and sophisticated, *everything* in it was *solid*, built to last and very well taken care of. The modesty of the interior made her smile to herself. It was as if he'd taken a decorating class from Otis. And just like Otis's apartment, there wasn't much to the living room other than a sofa, one recliner in the corner, a television of medium size, and a record player in the corner that sat on top of a small shelf that housed a modest vinyl library underneath it.

The focal point of the room was art. Where Otis had pictures of the legendary boxers on his wall, Israel had pictures of sweaty saxophone players leaning backward with their cheeks filled with air, guitar players with their heads down as they frowned while plucking the strings between their fingers. There was a darkness and a calm, a loss and an inspiration in Israel's pictures, the same sentiments she'd seen in Otis's pictures.

Chancey walked slowly through the living room, her eyes taking in the images of all the men she'd never seen before. She followed the photos around the room until she reached the entryway of the kitchen where they stopped. She turned back and looked at Israel, the man standing in a room surrounded by images of men she didn't know, yet she felt inspired by. Slowly, Chancey tilted her head to the side as she gazed at Israel and rubbed the tips of her fingers together in silent contemplation. "Not what I expected."

Following behind her slowly, watching her as she watched the walls, Israel stopped in the middle of the room, his hands in his pockets and his eyes fixed on hers. "What were you expecting?"

"Not sure. But not this."

Israel chuckled slightly to himself as he briefly lowered his eyes to the floor before resting his gaze again on Chancey's. "I'm not sure if I should be offended or flattered."

"Not offended."

Folding her arms across her chest as she leaned her back against the ledge of the countertop in the kitchen, her eyes danced around the room, taking in all the detail. "Your house is nice. It has a vibe to it, it feels like . . . like . . ."

Smiling from ear to ear as he looked around the room he'd decorated, Israel proudly nodded in agreement. "It's okay, I know what you mean. And you don't have to stand there like that, by the way. You can have a seat at the table, or we can sit in the living room if you want."

"In here's fine."

Chancey made her way to the high-top kitchen table, which was pressed against the wall, and Israel slowly strolled over to the space that Chancey had just vacated and retrieved two glasses from the cabinet. "Bourbon?"

"I'm more of a tequila drinker myself."

"Got that too."

With two glasses in one hand, and a bottle of tequila in the other, Israel made his way back to the table and sat across from Chancey. After pouring her a glass of tequila, he quickly made his way back to the counter and retrieved a bottle of bourbon and poured himself a glass. Once it was half full, he lifted his drink to Chancey and smiled. "Sante."

"Cheers."

After a few silent sips, Israel put his glass on the table. With an index finger on either side of the glass, he twisted it slowly as he looked at Chancey and waited for her to tell him the reason she was there. "When I left you that night in DC I didn't think I would see you again."

"See me in New Orleans, or see me in your house?"

"Both. And neither. I thought I'd never see you again *anywhere.*"

Clearly, she'd come to his home that evening to tell him something, something that she wasn't ready to say in that moment. To give her time, Israel finished his glass of bourbon and then poured himself another. "It's not safe for you here in Louisiana . . . and you know that."

"Yeah. I know."

The sensible response would have been yes, and yes is what she had said, but her acknowledging the danger that she was putting herself in put Israel ill at ease. "So, you came here to what? You're on some kind of suicide mission then?"

After finishing the last of the tequila in her glass, Chancey set the glass down softly and slowly slid it across the table toward Israel. "No, I wouldn't call it *a suicide mission.*"

"Then what would you call it then?"

"Not sure. Don't know what I'd call it. What I do know is that I'm tired. I'm tired of things happening to me—being taken from me. I've reached the point where I have nothing left. I have no one left. The last of what I had was taken from me when Mr. Otis took his last breath. So, I came here to take the only thing I could, vengeance. And if it's the only thing I can get, then it shall be mine. After all I've given, after all that he's taken, I'm owed at least that."

Chancey slowly shook her head as she put the glass up to her lips. "I've got nothing left. I'm here for that."

"So, you came down here on a revenge mission? You came down to fight?"

The cold, hollow look he'd seen before in her eyes made a swift reappearance. "No, not a fight. I came to set his whole world on fire."

Israel nodded as he silently ran his finger around the rim of his glass. There was nothing he could say to her in that moment, nothing he could tell her. She wasn't wrong with that she said. He knew the feeling and he understood the desire. He understood it well.

"I get it, Chancey, truly I do. But that man gave his life so that you could live yours. He wouldn't want you down here putting your life at risk to save a ghost."

"Otis didn't *give* anything. His life was taken from him. He was taken from me."

"Yes, he was, and I apologize. What I said came out wrong; I didn't mean it that way. What I mean to say is . . ." Israel sighed as he put his hand on his chest over his heart and looked solemnly at Chancey's emotionless face. "To his dying breath, that man protected you. Mr. Benjamin didn't want the same fate for you that the rest of your family had to succumb to."

"The rest of my family? And what did your computer tell you about the rest of my family, huh? That my dad, my dad was a criminal and a drug dealer who was murdered because of a drug deal gone wrong? Or that my mom—she was a dope fiend that over dosed? And that my brother—my br—" Letting the dead rest and rarely speaking their names had been her way of coping, but the thought of them, speaking their names, it put a lump in her throat she could just barely swallow. If it hadn't been for the tears that suddenly began to rush down her cheeks, the lump in her throat might not have gotten small enough for her to swallow, and she wouldn't have been able to continue. "And my brother, he died as a result of gang violence."

"Something like that."

Nodding as she pursed her lips together, Chancey pulled herself closer to the table and leaned in toward Israel.

"My father wasn't a criminal, maybe once upon a time he was, but he served his time and when he got out of prison, he never so much as jay-walked across a street. My father was a good man, a decent man; he was dependable and honest. His integrity is what got him killed. Trying to help the same man who got him arrested back in the day is what got him killed; trying to do the right thing got my father killed. The first time he went to jail it was to save his friend, *the one who would make it out the hood, but always be there to pour back into it,* or so he would say. That same friend made it out, got on the *right* side of the law, and became a cop. That *friend,* he did make it out, he made it out and never came back to give anything. Anytime I ever saw him come back it was with his hands open to take something else. He just kept taking from people who didn't have anything to give. And the last thing he took was more help from my father, and he's the reason my father got killed. And my mother, my mother she couldn't breathe without that man, it hurt her too much. Every night she tried to drown her sorrow in liquor, but every morning they'd come floating right back up to the surface, so she turned to drugs. She wasn't trying to get high; she was trying to make the pain stop. She just wanted it to go away. She wanted to be numb. And my brother, he would have made a great lawyer; that's what he was supposed to go to school for. I moved on from our parents' death, but he couldn't. He couldn't let it go. Once he graduated from high school and really started asking questions and filing paperwork looking into our father's murder, that was when my poor sweet brother ended up dead. Shot to death in the city he loved, in a neighborhood that loved him, by a gang no one can seem to name."

As the tears continued to fall, Chancey picked up her recently refreshed glass of tequila and drank it dry. "He tried to do things the *right way,* my brother. He was going to set the legal world on fire. He wasn't a fighter, not physically anyway, but he was ready to wage war on the system. I'm the fighter in the family." Smiling as she looked down in her cup, she shook her head. Everyone except Chancey herself had always seen her and thought of her as a fighter; this was the first time she saw herself as one. "So yes, I came down here for revenge. My family, they all chose their battles, and now I'm choosing mine, and this one is mine. I will not back down."

"I thought vengeance belonged to the Lord."

"The Lord owes me *something*. He has everything and everyone else. He owes me this one thing."

"You know the night Otis was murdered something was taken from me too." After taking the last gulp of bourbon in his glass, Israel set the glass down on the table and pushed himself out his seat and looked down at Chancey. "Hope. My hope was taken from me and my pride was crushed." Shaking his head as he mumbled to himself and made his way to the stove, Israel's body tensed as he grabbed a frying pan and set it on the burner. "I'ma fix us something to soak up some of this liquor. You like Cajun shrimp and grits?"

Chancey shrugged as she turned in her seat so that she could watch Israel. "Don't think I've ever had it before."

"I grew up on it; it's good."

"I'll try it."

As she watched Israel shuffle back and forth from the fridge to the stove, Chancey propped her elbow on the table and let her head rest in her hand. "Is that why you didn't say anything to DC Metro while you were there . . . your pride? Too proud to admit that the man you ride next to pulled one over on you? That your partner, the man you trust with your life, ain't nothing but a fraud and a murderer?"

"It's more to it than that."

The sizzling vegetables he was sautéing in the pan was the only sound that could be heard in the room for what felt like an hour. The silence between them was thick and heavy, but it wasn't uncomfortable; it was familiar to them both. "I didn't say nothing to DC Metro 'cause I was gonna handle it. That's how we do down here. And you're right, it hurts my heart and soul to know what Lorenzo's done, and to know that he's done it on my watch. It's more than just a blow to the ego. It's something else; I'm not sure how to explain it."

After throwing a few more ingredients into the cast iron skillet and shoving it back and forth over the fire a few times, Israel sat back down at the table and sighed as he poured himself some more bourbon. "I say, I lost my pride, not because I'm embarrassed. I say that because I've let people down without even knowing it all because of him."

With his right elbow propped on the table and the glass of bourbon in his left hand that sat resting on his knee, Israel shut his eyes and searched for a way to make Chancey understand. "A lifetime ago, back when I was a teenager, I was out in the streets in the Lower Ninth on my own . . . kind of. My grandmother, who raised me, she was from the Lower Ninth. She loved her neighborhood, and they loved her. She was the cornerstone of the area; you needed a kind word, some hard truth, food to eat, a place to keep a secret, she was that and more. She wasn't no saint, now; she had years of hard living before I came along, but she was a good woman. My mother left when I was really young, and so she took me in and raised me. She raised half the kids in the neighborhood whose parents couldn't or wouldn't."

She knew how the story would end. There was a flicker in his eyes as he paused and fished through painful memories and brought them to the surface. "What happened to her?"

"One day just outta the blue my mother showed up. She needed some money. I guess all her other tricks and schemes had finally run their course and she had nowhere else to turn, and so she went back home to her mama—my grandmother."

Something in Israel's somber smile at that moment eased every inch of tension in Chancey's body. She could relate to it, and so could he. There was something in the shared hurt deep down in their hearts that was healing.

As the image of his grandmother began to fade from his mind, so did Israel's smile. He was stuck somewhere between sad and stoic as he remembered everything he wished he could forget.

"My mother was a dope fiend in the worst kind of way, but I didn't hate her. I knew she loved me. She loved me enough to leave me the hell alone. Anyway, I wasn't there that day my mama came back to the house with some ol' friend of hers, but when I got outta school that evening, Shirlene was there sitting on my front porch waiting on me. We buried my grandmother three days later, and then they found my mother's body a week after that."

Still in his recollections, in a space in between sorrow and reverence, Israel smiled. "My grandmother was a bold woman. She never apologized for who she was or the things she'd done. She had no regrets, and she did what she had to do, however she had to get it done. But for me, she didn't want the same life. She wanted something different for me. *Roots and wings*, that's what she called it. She gave me a place to call home, somewhere I could feel safe and always come back to, but she didn't want me to stay there and be stuck; so *wings*, she gave me wings so I could fly. She made sure I went to school, got good grades, and headed in a direction that would get me somewhere other than where I was. *I* am where all my grandmother's prayers went."

Quickly finishing the last of what was in his glass, then rubbing his hands together quickly, Israel made his way back over to the stove. Spatula in hand, he looked down at the sizzling vegetables and gave them an absent-minded push. "I was not the man my grandmother raised me to be after she died. I don't know who I was. If I saw that boy now, I probably wouldn't recognize him. I stayed on a liquor-fueled rage for days, and when I found out who'd done it, after I found my mama's *friend*, I went after 'im. I didn't just kill 'im, I tortured 'im, and when it was over and done with, and I was at my lowest. When the reality set in that after all that I had done, she still wasn't coming back. I sat there covered in blood and waited for the police to come and drag me away, lock me up, and throw away the key. But after I don't even know how many hours passed, I looked up and saw Shirlene. I don't know where the body went. Hell, I don't even remember her getting me back home and getting the blood off me, but she did. I slept like the dead that night, but when I woke up, it was as if nothing had happened at all. Shirlene was in my kitchen the next morning scrambling eggs. She never said a word about how she found me and what she saw when she did, or what she did with the body afterward. Never said a thing about it, any of it. When I walked into the kitchen that morning, she turned and looked at me and told me to hurry my ass up and eat some breakfast before I got off to school that day. Every *left* I tried to make after that night, Shirlene was there to turn me around and send me in the other direction.

"My grandmother was there for Shirlene back in the day when Shirlene was in the midst of her darkest hour, and if it wasn't for me, I think Shirlene would have laid down next to my grandmother and died that night, but she didn't, she didn't because of me and the debt she owed my grandmother. Ever since that day, Shirlene has showed up for me in every way possible. Even when she couldn't be there physically for me, she made sure that someone was. Shirlene made sure that all debts were paid. The neighborhood owed my grandmother and Ms. Shirlene made sure they paid, and because of her, my entire neighborhood came together and got me through the worst days of my life. They never let me sell drugs, I never fought alone after that, there was always someone at my side without me having to call them, and they showed up for me without question or hesitation. They kept the devil at bay."

Bowls in hand, each one filled to the brim with creamy white grits and topped with succulent bright pink shrimp, Israel looked down at them and smiled as he made his way over to the table. He set down the bowls and looked at Chancey curiously. "Do you know what it's like to have people pray for you, Chancey? I had a whole neighborhood praying for me—it's a powerful thing. It's also a lot to live up to. Between my grandmother's legacy in that neighborhood and Shirlene's influence inside and outside of it, there was always someone watching my back, stopping me from going the wrong way. The people in that neighborhood looked out for me, the same way my grandmother had looked out for them. And to find out, I've been riding around with someone whose been doing them wrong, after all they did for me . . . it more than just hurts my heart, it's devastating. They prayed for me. I'm here today because of what they did for me back then, and I let them down. So, that's why I didn't say anything to the police in DC; that's why I haven't turned Lorenzo in to NOPD. I'm gonna fix this. I owe them that. Whatever I have to do to make it right, that's what I'm gonna do. They prayed for me, and I will not fail them a second time. I will not fail."

CHAPTER TWENTY

Night had quickly turned into day, and Chancey awoke in the guest bedroom of Israel's house to the smell of coffee and the sound of childish joy.

"Good morning."

As Chancey walked into the kitchen, she gave Israel a small grin and a slight nod. "Morning."

"I was about to leave a note for you. That was a lot of drinking we did last night. I didn't think you'd be up before I left. But I see you can hang with the best of 'em. Coffee?"

"Sanka?"

"How'd you know?"

Eyebrows raised and smile on her face, Chancey shrugged and shook her head as Israel stared at her in confusion.

"Yeah. Not too many folks around here drink Sanka, but I like it. It's strong and it'll get you through the day. Can't stand these little ass jars it comes in though. So, can I make you a cup?"

"Yes, please." As she slowly walked across the kitchen and looked around, Chancey thought about their conversation from the night before. Crossing her arms as she leaned against the wall by the refrigerator, Chancey peered out the window as she silently remembered Israel's words. "You're still going to work today?"

"Absolutely. If Lorenzo is there, then I'm there."

After handing Chancey her cup of coffee, which he sweetened to perfection, Israel sat down at the table and straightened his tie, then slowly and cautiously took a sip from his cup. "While I'm still on the *right* side of law, I wanna do as much as I can with the resources that I have access to. The stuff you told me in DC . . . tell me again. You were in shock before about Mr. Otis, but your head's clearer now. Tell me again."

Chancey took a deep breath as she leaned against the wall. She held on to the coffee mug with both hands, as if it was grounding her in the moment so she wouldn't fall into the reflections from her past. The warmth of the mug and the person who gave it to her, they were both keeping her steady. Deciding she was as ready as she was ever going to be, she looked over at Israel, and her brown eyes were already on the verge of tears by the very mention of Otis's name. So, she took another breath, and then a long sip of her coffee, and finally she gave Israel a small grin. It wasn't much, but it was all she had in that moment and she wanted him to know she was okay.

"I was in the corner store that morning for about ten minutes before everything happened. I was looking for some snacks Mr. Otis had told me about."

"You said that Victoria spoke to you directly before the shooting started?"

"Yeah. She came up to me by the snack cakes and pointed to the ones she liked the best, and she told me I should try them. I decided to take her advice and picked up two bags and was about to make my way to the chip aisle, but then I thought maybe I should ask her if she had any suggestions there too. But before I could say anything, that's when the four guys walked in."

She paused, looked down into her coffee, and smiled a smile so genuine it seemed like someone was in the mug smiling back at her.

"What? What's so funny?"

She reluctantly took her eyes off the mug, which was currently reflecting one of her fonder memories. Chancey looked over at Israel as she pushed herself off the wall and walked over to the table to sit with him. "I'd like to say it was *natural instinct*, me knowing where all the exits are whenever I step into a room, but it's not. It's my dad. He always said that I should walk away from confrontation when I could, but for the times I wouldn't be able to, for those times, he taught me how to fight. I was usually smaller than my opponents, but my dad taught me that boxing wasn't about who could throw the hardest punch. It was about agility—mental and physical agility. Who could move the quickest and who had the sharpest mind. Resilience and stamina are mental, and when you factor all those things together, you get a champ."

Nodding in agreement as he listened, the respect and admiration that Israel felt for the man he did not know and would never meet could be seen clearly all over his face.

"Anyway, I noticed the bathroom in the back when I walked in the store, so as they walked in and everyone either froze or tried to run out, I made myself small and backed slowly into the bathroom. But before I did, your friend, that Victoria lady, she told me they were there for her. She said that she would try and make sure no one else got hurt and that if she didn't make it that I should listen. She said that I should listen to everything and then make sure the truth came out. After she said that, I backed away and headed toward the bathroom. I figured it would have a window that

I could squeeze through, but the window was too high up and there was nothing below it that I could climb on to get to it, and then I realized that even if I could get to the window, it had bars on it, and so I gave up on that idea immediately. The ceiling, on the other hand, it was just as high, but it reminded me of the ceiling at the community center where Mr. Otis worked. A lot of the tiles had fallen at that place, so I knew it wouldn't be too hard to move the ones in the bathroom. Before I really had time to think it through, the shooting had started, and before I knew it, I was pushing myself off the top of the sink and into the ceiling."

Israel pushed his coffee to the side and gave Chancey his undivided attention as she spoke.

"Once I was in the ceiling, I wanted to crawl away from the bathroom just in case something looked out of place in there. I wanted to be far enough away from where I crawled in so that if they came in the bathroom to check if anyone was in there, and for some reason decided to reopen the ceiling tile and look in, they wouldn't see me right away. Once I could hear that I was directly over the store, I stopped and lay on the rafter and stayed as quiet as I could. The shooting had stopped, but I could hear people talking. One of the guys shooting was talking to your friend, the woman who told me about the snack cakes. I recognized her voice right away, and so I did what she told me to do . . . I listened. I could hear her telling them that she was *sorry*, that *it all went too far*; she said that she *didn't mean for any of it to happen*. She said she tried to fix it, she tried to get them out, but Lorenzo wouldn't let her. She kept screaming, 'Just ask Shirlene!' She said that Shirlene knew she tried."

"Did she say when she spoke to Shirlene?"

"No, nothing else about Shirlene. She just kept saying she was sorry and that she was a mother now, so she understood what they were going through, and she was trying to make it right but she couldn't make it right because Lorenzo wouldn't let her. She said, if she told the truth and got their friends out of jail, then Lorenzo would kill her, and she had a baby now to think of, so she couldn't do that. And that's when one of the shooters said they didn't care about her baby, that someone else's baby died in jail for something he didn't do because of her. They said all NOPD was good for was telling lies and taking lives. They wanted to know where the drugs were."

"Whose baby died?"

"I don't know."

"It's okay, I'll ask Shirlene about that one."

"This *Shirlene*, is she the same Shirlene from the story you told me last night?"

"Yes. One in the same."

Nodding as she took another sip of her coffee, Chancey sat the cup on the table and gave Israel a concerned look. "If he finds out that you know that he's a dirty cop and a murderer, he's gonna kill her. He's gonna kill Shirlene just to be cruel, just to drive you crazy."

"I'd sell my soul to the devil before I ever let that happen." Israel quickly exhaled the tension that was building up in his chest as he considered the thought of Lorenzo going after Shirlene. "So, did Victoria tell them where the drugs were?"

"She said that Lorenzo had three different trap houses scattered around the city, but she didn't know which one they were in. She said that the drugs her sister took the night she tried to drive out of town, they helped to start Lorenzo's drug business. She said that since then though, his business had quadrupled in size, and once his clientele started to grow, he stopped sharing information with her. And then she started apologizing again about the boy who died in jail, said she never meant for any of this to happen. She said it wasn't her fault, it was Lorenzo's fault."

"And then what happened?"

"One of them said it was her fault too. And then they shot her."

Israel jolted to his feet and left the room. When he returned, he had a piece of paper and a pen in his hand. "I'm giving you the address to Shirlene's bar down in the Quarter. I would prefer it if you stayed here until I got back, but if you have to leave, go there. Tell her I sent you. I'll stop by her place sometime around lunchtime to check in with her, but Chancey, please, please wait for me."

"Okay."

She made no promises. What she was saying *okay* to Israel didn't know, but what he did know was that, that *okay*, it was the best he was going to get.

***

His discussion with Chancey that morning had run longer than anticipated, and now he was running thirty minutes behind. But when he got to the precinct, much to his surprise, Lorenzo was running even later than he was.

Despite being surrounded by other officers, his partner wasn't there, and to him this meant he was alone. Israel decided to take advantage of his solitude by doing some research. The first file he pulled that morning was on Victoria's sister, Ruth Anne, affectionately known to all that knew her as Baby Ruth. The night of Baby Ruth's accident, the event that seemed to trigger this whole thing, Victoria was listed as a witness and the first one on the scene as far as the police force went. It was listed that she was responding to a distress call from her sister, and that she wasn't actually on the job when she first got there. In her statement she claimed the vehicle was already on fire when she arrived, and that she barely had time to pull Baby Ruth from the passenger seat of the vehicle before the car became fully engulfed in flames.

Also in her statement, Victoria claimed that her sister was in and out of consciousness and incoherent when she got to her. She claimed that *whoever* was driving the vehicle must've hit something with a considerable amount of force, which was likely what caused the car to burst into flames. When asked who she thought the driver might have been, Victoria said that when she spoke to Baby Ruth right before she had arrived, she could hear Baby Ruth's boyfriend in the background; he was a twenty-four-year-old local boy from the Ninth Ward. She finished by stating, that she was certain he was in the vehicle and was likely the one driving it.

Victoria's statement is what led to the arrest of three innocent men, one of them being the twenty-four-year-old local boy, the same boy who ended up dying in prison. Israel's curiosity about the other two men arrested with the young man intensified after he read the details of the report, but much to his dismay, he realized he had to hold off on any further inquiry because his partner had finally arrived. Lorenzo arrived almost an hour after Israel, but he looked as if he'd been working several hours longer. Lorenzo walked in and didn't say *hello* or *good morning* to anyone as he passed them. He plopped down at his desk and glared as his black computer screen.

After clicking a few buttons on his computer to close the file on his screen, Israel leaned back and swiveled his seat. "You all right, partner?"

"Yeah, yeah, I'm good."

Yawning as he massaged his forehead with his fingers and then quickly let his hands drop down to his desk, Lorenzo cleared his throat and gave Israel a quick nod. "Just a little tired. Did one of my late-night workouts is all. I probably just pushed it a little too hard."

"Okay."

"Looks like it's been a quiet morning. Don't look like I missed much of anything."

Israel sat up and let his elbows rest on his desk as he twirled a pen loosely between his fingers. "Nah, you ain't miss nothing. We ain't get no calls in this morning, yet. I've just been sitting here going through some backed-up paperwork."

"Yeah? Let's hope it stays quiet today and all the criminals stay in bed and off the streets. That way, we might just make it outta here on time, if not early."

"You tryna' get out early, you say? You got a date or something? You seeing somebody you ain't tell me about?"

"Oh see, here you go. Maybe, *maybe* I found somebody I don't mind sharing time with." Eyebrows raised as he smiled and rubbed his hands together.

Lorenzo shrugged his shoulder before turning sideways and turning on his computer. "Well, when can I meet her?"

"I don't know if we're at that stage yet. Soon though, I promise."

"All right, I'ma hold you to it."

For the next two hours, the two men worked across from each other in near silence. Aside from the occasional grunt *yeah,* or *uh-huh,* and *you finish that one,* there was very little said. It was barely lunchtime when Lorenzo jumped from his seat and took off down the hall without saying a word. When he returned back to his desk, he was not the same man he was when he left. He was visibly upset, so much so that Israel could see a thick vein pulsating in his neck.

"You all right, Lorenzo?"

"Uh—you know what? No. I think I really overdid it last night. I'm not feeling too good. I think I'm gonna head home and get some rest if that's okay with you, partner? I hate to do it to you, and if you need me here, you know I'll stay and I'll work through it, I just—"

"You know I got this. You go on and go home and get yourself some rest."

"You sure? You know, I'll stay if you need me. You just say the word."

"Lorenzo, I got this, man." Grunting as he got up from his seat, Israel quickly walked over to Lorenzo and gave him a quick pat on the back as he nodded toward the exit. "Don't worry about nothing going on here. You just go home and take care of you."

"Thanks, man. I owe you one."

Israel threw his palms up and smiled as he turned and walked away. Once he was back in his seat, he picked up his pen and began to turn it between his fingers again as he watched his 6'4" partner, who appeared to be in good health as far as he could tell, walk out the precinct too *sick* to finish his workday. Shaking his head in dismay as he watched Lorenzo leave, Israel clicked his tongue as he let the pen fall to his desk once again and he sighed. "Looks like a man on a mission to me. Far from sick."

Once Lorenzo was gone, Israel went back to researching. After going through all of Baby Ruth's known associates, he realized he knew more about Victoria, Baby Ruth, and the men she ran with than he knew about the man he worked with. He also knew that to get answers to the questions he never thought to ask, he couldn't just search NOPD's database; not only would it look strange that he was researching his own partner, but it would also be a waste of time. Clearly,

Lorenzo's jacket didn't reflect who he really was. To find out the truth about Lorenzo, he'd have to go to Shirlene. Shirlene was the woman who trusted him the least, which to Israel meant that she likely knew him the best.

Instead of taking a lunch that day, Israel hung around the precinct and got caught up on some paperwork. He also made some small talk with some of the other detectives. Mostly he chatted about Victoria's case. He tried to get a sense of who was truly saddened over Victoria's death, and who was remorseful and ashamed. He was looking for someone who might be a little unnerved and uncomfortable about the topic. But he found nothing among the men there that raised any red flags. The talk about Victoria's case quickly led to reminiscing about her past, and who she was, or who they thought she was while she was on the force . . . *a rising star*. The only one unnerved in the conversation was Israel, himself—lies, everything that they were remembering was a lie and it made him uneasy and angry.

After holding his tongue all day and keeping his emotions suppressed, by the time Israel got to Shirlene's bar that late afternoon, he was completely drained. It was just past four o'clock when he arrived. As he walked to the back of the bar to take his usual seat, he unbuttoned the top three buttons on his shirt and loosened his tie as he scanned the room and looked for the one face he knew wouldn't be there, but still held out hope would be.

"Who you looking for?"

With her hands full of empty glasses, Shirlene didn't bother to stop what she was doing; instead, she passed by Israel quickly and gave him a quick nudge with her shoulder to say hello and to let him know she was still listening.

"Thought a friend of mine might be here."

"A friend? What *friend* would be back here?"

As he pulled the barstool back so that he could sit down, Israel glanced over his shoulder to make sure Shirlene was on her way back to the bar, and he also wanted to give the room one last look to make sure Chancey really wasn't there. "I had a friend from outta town stop by my place last night. I asked her to meet me here today."

"And she ain't show up, or call? What kind of *friend* is she?"

"A friend in pain."

"Oh, I see." Shirlene shut her eyes as she nodded at Israel in understanding. "Well, sit and relax yourself. Let me pour you a drink. You look tired. You been sleeping all right?"

As he settled in, Israel looked across the bar and smiled at Shirlene as he rubbed his stubbly chin.

"What you up to? Why you smiling like that?"

"'Cause of you."

"Me? What did I do?"

"I ever tell you I love you, Shirlene?"

"No. And you ain't got to. I know you do."

As real and as mutual as the feelings were, the conversation made Shirlene uncomfortable. Neither ever felt the need to state the obvious. Certain words were just not said between them. They knew where they stood with each other, and that had always been enough for them. "Okay now, what's going on with you? You sending friends into my place, you come in and wanna talk about your feeling, this ain't like you. Somethings goin' on. So, tell me what it is."

"I'm good. I wasn't tryna worry you or nothing. I was just thinking about it on the way over here and I know, you know, that I love you, but I couldn't remember a time I ever told you that. Folks need to hear stuff like that every once in a while."

Leaning back against the counter, Shirlene folded her arms and pursed her lips together as she glared at Israel. "Uh-huh, I see. And you think, *I* need to hear it? Or is it your *friend* who needs to hear it? Or maybe it's just you—you just feel the need to say it to her?"

Puffing out his cheeks as he stared down at his glass, Israel held his breath briefly as he contemplated what Shirlene had said. "There's a certain kind of sadness, Shirlene . . . a certain kind of sadness that the soul cannot survive."

"Don't I know it."

"This friend of mine, she's had some hard days and some long, lonely nights. You ever just look at a person Shirlene and you just *know*?"

"Know what?"

Elbow on the bar and her chin resting in the palm of her hand, Shirlene tilted her head and peered through her partially squinted eyes at Israel as she waited for him to answer.

Even with his eyes closed, Israel knew Shirlene could see straight through him. He chuckled to himself as he tried to wipe the grin from his face. "Don't look at me like that now. And I know, you know exactly what I mean."

After regaining his composer and tossing back the rest of the bourbon in his glass, Israel leaned forward and rested his forearms on the ledge of the bar and interlocked his fingers. "You ever met someone who it felt like you been looking for your whole life and just ain't know it? Never knew them, never heard of them, but been looking for them for years, and when you find them, you find out you know them better than anybody else. This person you never met, you *know* them . . . you just fit together, like pieces to a puzzle. You know what I mean?"

"You talking about a soul mate?"

"No, I'm talking about—well, it does kinda sound like that now that you say it. But no, I mean . . . you know what? I don't know what the hell I'm talking about, just forget everything I just said."

"Mm-hmm." Chuckling to herself, she stood up straight and shook her head at Israel. "I know exactly what you mean." Shirlene smiled as she casually slapped the bar top with a rag. "You want me to pour you another one?"

After glancing quickly at the empty glass in his hands, Israel twisted his lips to the side and slowly shook his head. "No, I'm all right. I will take a beer though, keep it a little light tonight."

Before Shirlene could move, Israel was on his feet and making his way around the bar. "You all right, Shirlene. I'll get it."

It wasn't often that he stepped behind Shirlene's bar— no one besides Shirlene ever did—but Israel wasn't *nobody*, and he smiled as he walked past her and pulled out a bottle from the beer fridge.

For Israel to walk past her the way he did, Shirlene knew there was more he had to say, and whatever it was, was much more serious than the conversation they'd just had, and so she stayed where she was and watched him slowly approach her with his beer in his hand and a seriousness in his eyes.

Less than a foot away from her, Israel twisted the bottle cap in between his fingers as he took a sip and vacantly looked out at the bar. "I did some thinking today, Shirlene, and you know what? Outside of knowing where he went to school, and that he likes to work out, and how he spends his days patrolling the streets with me . . . I don't know nothing about the man. Told me once, his people was from the Ninth Ward. Used to be, you said you was from the Ninth and that was enough, you was family. Well, it ain't enough no more. It's ain't nothing really."

"Who says he's from the Ninth?"

Shocked, Israel put his beer down and furrowed his brows as he pursed his lips and tried to remember where he'd first heard the claim.

"That boy's people ain't from the Ninth, they from Tremé."

"How long you known that?" he asked.

"Since the first day he stepped his big ass foot in this Quarter."

"Tremé ain't nothing but a bus ride away, Shirlene. If that's where he's from, why not just say that? One place ain't that much different than the other when you grow up with nothing."

"I'll tell you like this. That boy is from Tremé. He ran away from where he came from after his mother was murdered. Folks 'round there call him Jordi. They don't know who this *Lorenzo* person is."

"Jordi? Okay. How'd his mama die?"

"Shot. Say it was a drug deal gone wrong. Only witness was her son, Jordi, who went missing right around the time her case ran cold."

"You think he killed her?"

"I think it's a little strange a boy don't stick around to mourn his mama. Even stranger that he reappears as a man she didn't raise. Makes you wonder why Jordi ran to Lorenzo. Can't say too much about Jordi, but at least we know where he's from and who his people are. Can't say the same about *Lorenzo*; don't know nothing about who he is or where he's been."

Shirlene looked down at the floor as she shuffled her feet. "This friend of yours, you say she's good at hiding. It's always been my experience that those people who run from the truth, they're usually the best ones to find it. I believe your friend is in pain, but she's here for a reason. She ran from this city once before; she ran away from telling the truth. If she's back, then she's back for a reason. You wanna find answers, you follow her, she knows the way. I'd bet my bar on it."

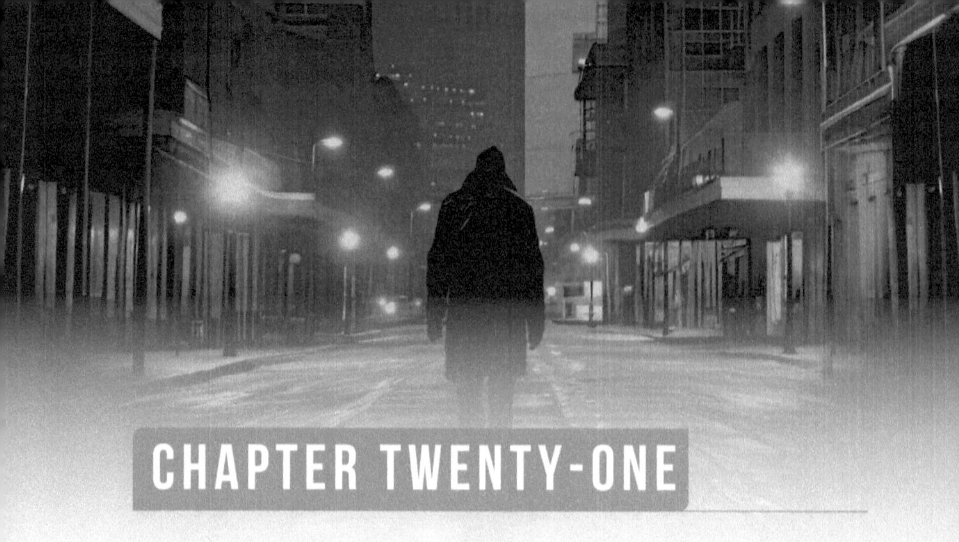

CHAPTER TWENTY-ONE

Scratching his head as he walked up the steps to his home, Israel thought intently about what the next step would be in his effort to bring down Lorenzo.

Lost in his own thoughts as he walked inside his house, the soft creak of the floorboards snapped him to attention and sent his heart racing into a panic.

"Jesus, Lord, you're still here. You damn near scared me half to death." Slowly releasing his grip on his side arm that he had very nearly pulled out and drawn on Chancey, Israel sighed with relief at the sight of her.

"I can see that I did." Spatula in hand as she leaned back against the counter somewhat amused by Israel's reaction, Chancey smiled to herself as she silently waited for him to get comfortable. "Why wouldn't I be here? You asked me to stay, didn't you?"

"Yeah. I know I did. I just didn't think that you would. I thought if I saw you at all today it would be down at Shirlene's place, but when I got there and didn't see you and she told me that you hadn't been in, I figured you took off again."

"And gone where? To who?"

Her words fell on his chest like bricks. If he had the answer to her question, he wouldn't have been able to say what it was, not in that moment; she had knocked the wind right out of him without even trying.

"Please don't look at me like that. I don't need your pity, Israel."

"I'm not. It's not pity. It's—It's . . . you know what? I don't even know what to call it, but I promise you, it ain't pity."

Feeling a little lighter, spiritually and physically, Israel smacked his hands together and rubbed them quickly as he got up from the table and headed to the fridge. "I'ma have myself a beer, you want one?"

"Please."

"What you over there cooking anyway?"

"Just a little bacon jam to put on the burgers."

"Bacon jam? Where you learn to make something fancy like that?"

The idea that she was doing something *fancy*, amused her more than the shock she'd given him when he came in. As she laughed, the beer she'd been attempting to take a sip of missed her mouth completely and rolled down her chin. "Me? Fancy? Now, that's one that I haven't heard before. I've been called a lot of things, but never that."

Still laughing as she wiped her mouth with the back of her hand, she shut her eyes and inhaled deeply as she reached into her memory for an explanation. "Otis. He showed me. He was always on me about not knowing how to cook, and he wasn't wrong. God knows I burn almost everything I try and make. But this, this is the one thing I always get right. We made all types of jams together, and we pickled every vegetable he could find. And this was despite me telling him that not all things need to be pickled and that vinegar does not make everything better or last longer, and even if it did last, who would want to eat something that tasted nasty, like broccoli. Who in the hell pickles broccoli?"

Frowning in disgust and laughing at the same time, neither one of them could take a sip of their drinks at that point.

"Yeah, I'd have to agree with you on that. But your Mr. Otis, he sounds a lot like my Shirlene. She always in that bar making her own liqueurs. Least that what she calls 'em. I keep tryna tell her that vodka ain't gonna turn every fruit peel into a good liqueur. But she don't listen."

Israel slowly slid his finger down the side of the bottle, allowing his fingers to make trails in the condensation. He thought about the conversation he had with Shirlene earlier that evening, and as he looked at the bottle and pursed his lips, he gave it an agreeing nod as if it had repeated what Shirlene had said and he knew what he had to ask. "Hey, Chancey, what is it *exactly* that you came down here to do?"

After tossing the patty of meat that she had in her hand into the hot pan on the stove, Chancey silently moved over to the sink and washed her hands. Her back still turned toward Israel and her hands full of soap, she sighed as she shrugged her shoulders.

"Guess I came down here to take everything from him, the same way he took everything from me."

"And how's that? How you planning on doing that?"

Folding her arms across her chest, she turned to face Israel. Chancey looked him in his eyes and firmly held his gaze. "Violently and without remorse."

She meant what she said, and Israel knew it. But how she intended to do what she claimed she was going to do, that was what he still didn't know but was very eager to find out. "Don't take this the wrong way, but he's an officer of the law, Chancey. He's trained and certified by the state of Louisiana, and you, you're—"

"And me, I'm just an uneducated orphan, hood rat who's in way over her head?"

"That's not what I was going to say."

"Well, what then? I'm listening. What is it that you were going to say, that I shouldn't take the wrong way?"

"You're a grieving, out of towner, on a mission of revenge all by herself; while Lorenzo, he's got an entire force behind him. Not to mention a life and a crew you don't even know about. In my opinion, you need to know your enemy in order to defeat 'em, and you don't know Lorenzo." Israel picked up his beer and took a long hard sip before putting it firmly back down on the table. "Hell, I don't know Lorenzo."

"You know the difference between a criminal and a con?"

Surprised by what seemed to be a change in the conversation they were having, Israel shook off his momentary confusion and nodded. "Yeah, I know the difference very well. Criminals are usually young and dumb, repeat offenders without a code or any sense of loyalty. And a con—a real convict knows how to work the system, how to work within the system they're in. They've got rules and their own code of honor. But what does any of that have to do with anything?"

Grinning as she flipped the burgers in the pan, Chancey glanced over her shoulder at Israel and smiled. "Otis was a con . . . like my dad. Good men who did some fucked-up things, but good men nonetheless. A lot of the wrong things they did, they did for the right reasons and they usually weren't doing it for themselves."

Chancey grabbed two plates from the cabinet and began to put the pieces of the burger together. Israel silently sipped his beer and waited for her to finish.

"When Otis got the call from Lorenzo after I first got back home, he got real nervous and then when I told him what happened—forget about it, he was on it after that." Satisfied with her work, Chancey picked up the plates and turned to face Israel. "Eventually, all debts come due. And like I said, the dirt my dad and Otis did back in the day, it was rarely ever for themselves. So, to get me out of trouble, Otis called in a few debts that were owed to him."

After carefully placing both plates down on the table, Chancey sat to the side of Israel and gently slid his plate toward him. "I know my enemy, Israel. I know him well. Otis would not have settled for less."

Too engrossed in what she was saying to touch his food, he silently watched as Chancey took a bite of her burger. As he waited for her to finish what was in her mouth, he quickly got up from his seat and got two more beers.

"Everyone thinks that I gave up boxing when my dad died, but that's not true. I never gave up boxing; I gave up competing. I never gave up training. The owner of the gym where I train at, he owed my father a debt. He wouldn't even have that gym if it weren't for my dad. Him, my dad, and this guy Eugene, they grew up together. My dad did time for both of them. And because of him, one of them went legit and became a business owner and opened a gym, and the other got out the neighborhood completely and became a cop. They both owe their lives to my father; their debt didn't die with him. They're repaying me. They don't owe me anything, but they owed him everything, and they're making good on the promises they made to him. They're standing by their word."

As she took a sip of her beer, she nudged the edged of Israel's untouched plate toward him. "What's wrong? Not hungry?"

"No. No, I am. I was just listening. Listening and thinking." Israel quickly picked up his burger and took a bite, raising both eyebrows as he chewed and nodding as he eyed the burger in his hand. Cheeks full, he smiled and nodded at Chancey giving his approval. "This is good. Bacon jam, you say?"

"Mm-hmm, bacon jam." Grinning as she took another sip of her beer, she was filled with pride at how well she remembered everything Otis had taught her as she proudly watched Israel take another bite. "So, while you may not know Lorenzo, I know him well. He's a criminal. And I happen to know a cop, who lives like a con, and spends his days hunting criminals. I know exactly what type of man—criminal—Lorenzo is."

"An honorless, disloyal fool who is only out for himself."

"Exactly."

Despite starting last, Israel finished his burger first. "Okay, so you know him better than I do, that still don't mean you can beat him." Rubbing his hands together as he looked down at his empty plate, Israel adjusted himself in his seat. "As much as you might train, I promise you, he trains harder. Lorenzo works out every day, plus he's three times your size. And he carries a gun."

"Like I told you before, training isn't just physical, it's mental too. Just because he's bigger than me and has more education than me, doesn't mean he's faster or smarter. I told you, I came down here to take everything from him, but I never told you he would see me coming."

At this point, Israel knew that Chancey wasn't going to share her plans with him. She trusted him to some extent, but not completely.

Once she was done with her burger and had collected both empty plates from the table, Israel silently watched

Chancey walk over to the sink and turn the water on. As if someone had lit a match underneath him, Israel jumped to his feet and made his way over to her and quickly reached around her waist and shut the water back off.

"Chance, you're a guest in my house. You don't have to do the dishes. Leave them there, they'll be fine."

Spinning around quickly, and now nearly nose to nose with Israel, Chancey put her hand up over her mouth in an attempt not to laugh in his face.

"What? What's so funny?"

"Nothing, it's just, the way you said that just now, *Chance, leave them there.* I don't know, it felt like—kinda felt like home."

"Is that a bad thing?"

"No. I just wasn't expecting it. It felt good, it felt familiar. Like I wasn't alone."

"You're not alone."

"Well, not right now. I know that. I didn't mean literally—"

"I know what you meant. And you are *not* alone."

Right then, in the middle of all the chaos and confusion going on in their lives, it was there in that familiar moment that the two of them were able to find a calm and quiet place in each other. With his hands on her waist, Israel pulled Chancey closer to him until their bodies were firmly pressed together. Her hands grabbed the base of his neck as their mouths met exactly in the middle of the small space that was left between their faces.

They fit. Their bodies shared memories with each other that their minds did not. Their movements were instinctive and intense, passionate and effortless. As one of his hands slid up the front of her torso, the other was lifting the shirt over her head. As he caressed the curve of her waist and traced the corners of her mouth with his tongue, she pushed back the sleeves of his unbuttoned shirt and held on to his bare shoulders as he lifted her from the ground. Once her legs were securely wrapped around his waist, and he was comfortable holding the weight of her body in the palms of his hands, they paused and looked at each other. They both knew in that moment that they had finally found each other, and the weight they'd both been carrying around with them all their lives suddenly went away. Overcome with relief, Israel inhaled deeply and took in the air from Chancey's mouth. She slowly shut her eyes and let her forehead fall forward and softly rest against his.

He carried her out of the kitchen and into his bedroom. His hands firmly held the backs of her thighs as Chancey kissed his entire jawline and then rubbed her face against the side of his. Once they finally reached his bed and he laid her down, Israel gently laid his body against hers and rested on top of her, pressing his palm firmly against the headboard with one hand and slowly caressing the side of Chancey's face with the other. Israel looked down at her and was completely overcome with desire and passion in a way that he didn't know he could be.

"You—are not alone."

There might have been more he had to say, but the statement seemed to be all he could manage to say in that moment, but his words hit her ears like the wind. His words were soft and steady, gentle enough to float a feather, yet powerful enough to bring down a deeply rooted tree. Before he could say anything else, Chancey reached up with both hands and pulled his face to hers. She kissed him like he'd meant it, like he meant every single word of what he'd said, and deep inside she knew he did. She knew he meant it, as surely as she felt it.

She wanted to say something; she wanted him to know that for the first time in a long time she didn't *feel* alone. But she didn't say anything. She didn't utter a single word. She was literally speechless. And since she couldn't speak, since she couldn't tell him what she was feeling, she showed him in the only way she could by kissing him long and hard and deeply. She kissed him with every inch of her soul, hoping that he would see that she didn't feel alone anymore, and that she was grateful, so very grateful to him that he had found her. She kissed him until all the breath she had nearly left her body, and when she needed air, when she opened up her mouth to take a breath, she felt him thrust himself inside of her and she inhaled every part of him. She took in every inch of his manhood, cradled every ounce of his weight, and took the breath from his mouth straight into her lungs. With his breath she felt as if could breathe again, she could finally *be* again. "Oh God—*Thank you. Thank you.*"

They fit. They fit together in ways words could not convey and only their bodies could understand. And when they were done, when both of them were thoroughly drained, they lay there silently facing each other, embracing one another in the darkness where they had both found love for the first time.

***

The next morning arrived and brought with it a sense of contentment, the likes of which Israel had never seen before. He could see the sun that morning before he even opened his eyes. The warmth of it brought a smile to his face. Before he could settle into this newfound feeling, he realized he was in the bed alone, but before his heart could start racing, he felt a small nudge at his foot and he smiled again, wider than he had before. He didn't need to open his eyes and see her to smile, just knowing that she was still there, that she hadn't run, that he was not alone, it brought him more joy than he could have asked for.

"And what are you smiling about this morning?"

"Sounds like you're smiling too. Guess we both just woke up happy."

Smiling back at him as she slowly crawled back into the bed, Chancey let out an unintentional snort, which was quickly followed by a carefree giggle. "And how do you know I'm smiling? You haven't even opened your eyes yet."

The sound of her happiness made him smile more. He slowly opened his eyes and looked up at her. He chuckled to himself and winked at her. "And you're still smiling."

"I made you coffee."

"I see that and thank you."

Chancey sat back down on the bed and got comfortable once again by Israel's side. She pulled her legs up to her chest and looked down at Israel, smiling as she rocked her body forward until her lips were touching his. Now feeling just as content as he looked, she lay back down next to him and draped one arm around his still-naked body and buried her face into the side of his bare chest. She shut her eyes and searched her memory of the night before behind her closed lids and hummed the lyrics to "One and a Million You" softly to herself while playing and replaying each moment of the previous night. The repetition of the song, along with the replaying of memories in her mind, it was like she was etching the moments on her heart, scarring herself again and again to make sure the memory would never fade. As if he could see what she was doing, with his eyes still closed and with a smile still on his face, Israel reached down and clasped his hand around hers.

He reached for her. He offered her his hand and she took it, and he was relieved that she did, but still—he flinched. He flinched because, for him, good didn't last long, and this . . . this was more than just good; this moment was everything for him.

"Chancey?"

She slowly opened her eyes and rolled over to face him. She searched his face and waited for his lips to part and say something, but they didn't. His lips didn't move. He didn't say anything. She followed his gaze with her eyes, until her gaze rested with his on their interlocked hands. "I know."

Her statement that morning had been just as powerful as his had been the night before. She knew exactly what he couldn't ask, just as he knew exactly what she couldn't promise. She couldn't not go after Lorenzo, she couldn't just stay there with Israel, and she certainly couldn't promise that she wouldn't get herself killed; she definitely couldn't promise that. And since she couldn't promise, and he knew better than to ask, instead of speaking they just lay there together, side by side, hand in hand, each one longing to hear the words that they knew the other could not say.

CHAPTER TWENTY-TWO

"Saint Claude Ave . . . Jourden Ave." Shirlene looked across the table at Israel intently. Worry filled her face the same way liquor filled a glass.

As he carefully squeezed a lemon over the oysters in front of him, Israel searched his mind for clues as to what it was Shirlene was talking about. Zeke's restaurant wasn't their favorite place to eat, but it was quiet and out of the way of things. Close enough to the Quarter without being in it.

As he studied the now empty shell that he'd slurped clean, Israel shrugged in defeat. The importance of what Shirlene was trying to convey was not lost to him. He knew the names had meaning; he just needed more information than what she was providing.

She reached her hand toward the platter of oysters between them and took a breath. "Them two fires last week. One was on Saint Claude, and the other was on Jourden."

"They look good today. Must'a caught these not too long ago." Zeke's didn't have the best food in the area, not for their taste; for them, the best food came straight from Shirlene's kitchen. They never went there for the food, not really. They went there for the quiet and to discuss things they felt couldn't be said anywhere else. They respected each other's positions in society. Shirlene never wanted to jeopardize Israel's career, and Israel never wanted to be the one to put Shirlene's honor in question. Zeke's allowed them to lean in close to each other and speak in hushed voices and half sentences without anyone else's eyes on them accusing them of being *up to something.*

"Your friend still in town?"

As if the oyster at his lips had just grown a new shell and shut closed on him, Israel quickly jerked it away and let it fall to the table. "I believe they are still in the area somewhere."

Quickly wiping the corners of his mouth, Israel silently waited for Shirlene to explain. Since the day that Chancey had arrived, Israel hadn't wanted to be away from her. But now, here at Zeke's with Shirlene, knowing that something bad was brewing on the horizon, the feeling that he'd had since she arrived, it suddenly filled him completely and overwhelmed him with the desire to get back to her right away. But he wouldn't rush her, he would never rush her. Shirlene had always been his lighthouse, and it was clear to him that this meeting was his light in the window. However long it took, he would wait and he would listen because he knew that her light and her counsel was to always to guide him in the right direction and keep him safe.

"Your friend—did they say where they was staying?" As she smacked her lips together and quickly sucked the last of the juice from the shell in her hand, Shirlene frowned as she shook her head and sucked her teeth while she looked across the table at Israel. "'Cause, I swear I thought you told me that they might be staying on Saint Claude or Jourden—thought they knew somebody over there . . . or what was the name of that other place you said they might go? What street?"

Shirlene looked over at Israel and raised both eyebrows. After wiping her mouth, she quickly threw her used napkin down on the table and shook her head. "Well, that wasn't bad—wasn't good neither."

Israel raised his hands toward their waitress and signaled for the check. Thankfully the waitress was quick, and no sooner had she dropped the check on the table did Israel in turn drop his cash. It had all finally come together for him. All the things Shirlene had said and, more specifically, what she had not said. He knew exactly what she meant, and once she was satisfied her message had been received, they both silently agreed that it was time to go.

They exited the restaurant together, side by side in silence, like two strangers who happened to be in the same place at the same time.

"Okay, I'll see ya." Shirlene swatted her hand in Israel's direction before opening the door to the dark green Cadillac that was parked in the handicap spot right up front.

Israel gave a slight nod in her direction before heading into the parking lot toward his car. Once inside, he put the key in the ignition and sat there. Instead of turning the key, he leaned back against the seat and sat silently in the dark. As he sat there with his mind racing, he taped his fingers intently on his center console. After several minutes of sitting there tapping and nodding to himself repeatedly, he huffed and shook his head. "Not this time, no sir, not this time." Still shaking his head, Israel quickly leaned forward, twisted the key in the ignition, and exited the parking lot.

Summers in New Orleans were brutal. August was especially hot and humid, and although it was night, the temperature was still well above eighty degrees. The heat was something Israel truly believed no one ever became accustomed to, but that night, it barely phased him. As he drove home with his windows rolled all the way down, with the barely there gust of humid sticky air hitting his face, he was completely unbothered. It wasn't until he pulled into his driveway that he began to sweat.

Making his way up the steps to the front door, he looked into the front window of his home and hesitated. The inside was dark. The only light that could be seen was the automatic light in the kitchen that was set on a timer and was too dim to really illuminate anything but was just enough light to keep him from walking into pure darkness.

Once inside and standing in the living room, stillness and silence bombarded his sense all at once, and reluctantly he inhaled deeply and took in all the disquiet in the room. There was a solemnness in that house that hadn't been there when he left, but it was there now, and it was currently sending shivers up his spine. When he finally did exhale, the sound of his breath and soft footsteps took the place of the soundlessness and gave life to the dark and quiet night.

"You made it back safe, I see." He could feel her before he could see her. Even without the footsteps, her presence was palpable.

"And so have you. But, between the two of us, you're the one who looks like he's trying to claw his way out the wrong end of a bottle." Chancey slowly stepped out of the dark hallway and into the dimly lit entrance of the living room. She studied Israel and the weariness he seemed to have brought back with him.

"Had dinner with an old friend."

"I don't have any of those, but if the look on your face is all I have to go by, I feel pretty confident in saying, it doesn't look like I'm missing out on anything."

As dark as the inside of his house was, it wasn't dark enough for Israel. Before another word was spoken between them, he made his way around the living room shutting every blind and pulling closed every curtain. It was highly unlikely that anyone would just show up to his home unannounced, or that a passerby would look through one of his windows and get a glimpse of Chancey and recognize her, but still, he went around and checked the latches on the windows that he never unlocked, pulled at the curtain he'd already closed, and then surveyed everything from another angle to make sure it couldn't be seen through before he finally decided that it was okay to turn the lights on.

With his body a little more relaxed than it had been from when he first got home, Israel slowly and silently made his way over to where Chancey stood. Once they were toe to toe and nose to nose, with no space between his body and hers, he took in a deep breath and inhaled all the unspoken cold, hard truths that lay between them.

"You don't have to worry about me. I know what I'm doing."

Sighing, he grabbed Chancey around the waist and pulled her closer. He gently kissed her forehead before softly brushing the side of his cheek against hers and softly whispered over the despair that was trapped in his chest. "He's gonna come after you."

"Maybe." Chancey locked her eyes on Israel's and smiled at him as best she could before giving a slight shrug. "He's gonna kill me." The tone in which she spoke had the same level of calmness as she had confidence in herself and her intentions. "It's okay, Israel. I know. I knew that before I got here. He's gonna kill me."

It wasn't okay, but she also wasn't wrong. If Lorenzo didn't kill Chancey, he was certainly going to at least try, and if he failed, then he would just keep trying. He would never stop.

With his head still resting against hers, Chancey smiled again. This time it was real, this time she meant it. As she smiled and leaned forward, she kissed Israel's closed eyelids. She kissed him slowly and softly all over his face until her lips found his. She could feel his heart in tune with hers and his breath in rhythm with her own. As she listened, she held on to him tighter as she slowly and reluctantly lifted her cheek from his until they were once again nose to nose. Face to face, with lips touching but barely kissing, Israel slowly opened his eyes and looked at Chancey, and his gaze nearly took her breath away. Before her lungs could give out on her, before she had a minute to think, Chancey tilted her head to the side and pressed her lips firmly against his partially open mouth and kissed him as if it were the last time. She kissed him like she'd never see him again, and it felt so right, and so good . . . and it hurt like hell all at the same time.

The swirl of emotions that had him tongue tied all rushed to the surface the second her lips touched his: desire, anger, desperation, love, loss. All the emotions he'd been fighting with within himself all came crashing down on him, and in the midst of the storm inside of him, he did the only thing he could think to do, the only thing that made sense to him in that moment: he kissed her back, he loved her back.

His head was clear for the first time that evening. He only had one thought in his mind—love. In the dark with the woman he might never see again. They had made their way to his bedroom without effort, without light, without even knowing they were moving. Chancey held on to Israel with her legs around his waist, her arms around his neck, and her lips pressed against his until they had made their way into his bedroom and he was laying her down on the bed. Israel's breathing became shallow, and his heartbeat louder as Chancey's hands moved from his neck to his ribcage as she caressed each bit of flesh she touched. The moment was incomparable to anything either had ever experienced before. It was as if they were saying, *I love you* for the first time, while all the while bidding each other farewell.

As their bodies rubbed against each other and their hands fumbled around in desperation trying to get rid of the clothing that kept their flesh from touching, all of a sudden, as if he'd been set on fire, Israel jolted to his feet and quickly ripped off his shirt as if it were scorching his skin. His broad chest was warm, and his chest hairs clung to him from the sweat that was beading up along his body from the heat that was radiating through him.

Passion and impatience brought Chancey to her knees; the half a minute it was taking for Israel to get undressed was too much time for her. She placed both of her palms against his sweaty chest, while Israel leaned forward, grabbed both sides of her face, and gently pulled her lips to his again. The feel of his thumb as it rubbed gently around the base of her neck fueled Chancey's lust, and her hands that had been clawing at his pecks were now desperately grabbing and clenching at his shoulders and his back.

The longing and the lust that Israel felt, his need to be with her in that moment, was like nothing he'd ever experienced before. The heat between them felt hotter than any day he'd ever experienced living in Louisiana. But this heat he shared with Chancey, he enjoyed this heat, and he wanted more of it. If he could stay in that moment with her—his whole body on fire, every nerve inside of him open and exposed—he would have stayed there like that forever.

Completely naked, exhausted, out of breath, and at the same time exhilarated and eager, Israel kissed and nipped at Chancey's breasts as her thighs pressed against him. The wetness from between her legs only added to the heat radiating throughout his body. He hovered over her body, her legs tightly wrapped around his waist, and he stared down at her and watched as she kissed and licked his chest until her tongue found the softest part of his throat and caressed it. Her mouth sucked it until his eyes rolled shut with pleasure, and his arms that were holding him up trembled and threatened to collapse. He couldn't tell if it was ecstasy or delirium he was feeling just then. The only thing he knew for sure was that it felt like his entire soul had been set on fire.

They were physically and mentally drained, but never had either felt so content and so complete than they did in that moment. With sweat being the only thing covering their naked bodies, they lay there tangled up in each other, panting as if they had just run a marathon and won. They now both knew what love felt like—so they had won; only the race wasn't over yet. There was a brief moment of stillness between them, a quiet place that they both seemed to have found at the same time, and they looked into each other's eyes and shared that moment of knowing. Israel slowly slid into Chancey, and as she gasped with pleasure, they clung to one another, their heads both spun with ecstasy, adrenaline, fear, and love.

CHAPTER TWENTY-THREE

She may not have started this fire, but she knew she was the cause of it. As the flames danced in the glossy reflectiveness of her eyes, Chancey took a deep breath and quickly weighed her options. She could do nothing and walk away and let the building burn, or she could go in. It took her less than a full minute to decide. Her choice: she would absolutely put her plan and herself in harm's way to save a life . . . to save *two* lives.

She stood there staring down the flames, and her heart began to pound. She knew this opponent better than she knew the one she'd come to town for, but her immense knowledge of the imminent danger she was in didn't deter her. The image of Israel's serene sleeping face filled her mind and made her steady and gave her strength. She flinched knowing the hurt he'd be feeling when he would wake up and find her gone. Knowing she would be causing him pain and wouldn't be able to do anything about it was reason enough to drive her inside the building. She couldn't just stand there. She couldn't just walk away and leave Israel to mourn over everything he'd lost that night. If she could prevent him from feeling this specific loss, this all-encompassing sorrow, then she would do whatever she could to prevent it no matter what the cost.

As she cautiously crawled inside the window she'd been staring through, her eyes darted around the dark smoky room, confirming that the coast was clear before she pulled her entire body inside.

"Shirlene?" Whispering in earnest above the smoke, Chancey crouched down as low to the floor as she could get as she tried to make her way to the area she'd last seen Shirlene.

"Shirlene?"

While the flames inside the bar had yet to reach their full potential, the smoke on the other hand was excelling and compromising Chancey's vision as well as her breathing. Surrounded by smoke and finding it difficult to breathe, the confidence that Chancey had outside the bar—the hope and determination that was within her—all began to fracture and fade. It was less than two hours ago that she as lying next to Israel, her naked body pressed against his as she ran her fingers softly up and down his jawline while he peacefully slept. It was less than two hours ago that she realized that she had finally found someone she wanted to live for and with. It was less than two hours ago that her suicide mission fueled by revenge turned into a mission of sacrifice and sorrow. The same man she could imagine spending her life with had become the one man who she was willing to sacrifice her life for.

As the smoke attacked her from above, defeat began to rise and attack her from below, but before either could truly take hold of her, her ears picked up on a sound that overwhelmed her with joy and far outweighed anything else she was feeling inside. It was the soft clanking of metal against metal, and the sound was louder than the flames that were growing larger and angrier. The soft whisper of the metal tapping was sharp enough to cut through the smoke that had been clouding her eyes and gave her the light she needed to see.

She had been right. Shirlene was less than five feet away from her. She was bleeding and in bad shape but she was there. She was still alive, still banging the metal mixing glass in her hand against the bottom rail of her bar. She was still fighting to stay alive.

"Hold on just a little bit longer, Shirlene. Hold on."

***

The ringing of his phone was as sobering as it was painful against his ears. Chancey was gone, and he didn't need to open his eyes to see that. He could feel it, and the knowledge of that—that reality—hurt him more and hit him harder than anything else had in years.

"Saint James."

The quiet in his room seemed louder than the voice on the other end of the phone, but then his heart picked up on something that his mind had yet to comprehend. His chest got tight and his heart began to pound and seemed to get louder and louder with each beat as he processed what he'd been told. "Wait, what was the address? Say it again."

Anxious and confused, Israel sat upright and searched around his dark and lonely room and tried to find reason and understanding.

"You mean Shirlene's place? Someone set Shirlene's place on fire?"

He didn't need details; all he needed was confirmation. He needed confirmation that what he thought he heard is

173

what had actually been said, and once confirmation came, he was dressed and out the door.

The ride to the bar was a blur. By the time he'd made it to the front entrance of the building, the last flame was being extinguished.

"Crazy ain't it? All these fires popping up around town all of a sudden . . . kinda like the way an unexpected guest pops up at your house on a holiday—uninvited and unannounced. Makes you angry, don't it?"

He knew what it looked like. He knew what it looked like and what would be reasonable to believe, but Israel was never one to be led. As he slowly turned toward the voice coming from behind him, Israel took several slow breaths. His nostrils flared in anger the same way a bull's did right before it charged.

Standing face-to-face with Lorenzo, each one looked at the other with the same sense of knowing, a shared understanding that neither would say aloud. They wouldn't speak there, not there in the middle of the sidewalk with dozens of listening ears around. Israel clenched his fists at his sides as he silently stared down the man he once trusted with his life.

"Guess luck was on the old girl's side tonight. They say wasn't nobody inside. Although, they won't know for sure 'til they're able to do a full sweep, but they don't think nobody was in there." The right side of Lorenzo's mouth pulled into a slight grin, which he quickly released as he arrogantly raised an eyebrow at Israel.

"Yeah, real lucky, I guess." Lorenzo had meant to hurt him and to send him a message. Israel had received the message, but the blow it had delivered had not been the one that Lorenzo had intended. As Israel unclenched his fists and jammed his tense hands into his sweatpants pockets, he took a step closer toward Lorenzo. "It takes a real soulless son of a bitch, coward of a man—if you could call him a man—to go after an old woman like that. Burn her alive in her own bar . . . a coward and a fool."

With their eyes fixed on each other and their silent glares saying everything their mouths could not, the thick tension between them that was clouding the air around them was abruptly sliced through by the ringing of Lorenzo's phone. Smirking at Israel as he turned his back on him and answered the call, Lorenzo slowly walked away from the bar and away from Israel without saying another word and walked back to his car. Once inside his vehicle, he shot Israel one final glance of contempt and a devious grin before he turned the key in the ignition and drove off.

Israel's heart was heavy, and his mind was racing as he stared at the burnt building in front of him and watched the smoke fill the night sky. He wanted to go after Lorenzo. He wanted to follow him and put his hands around his neck and choke the life from his lungs the same way he had imagined the smoke choking Shirlene. But he couldn't follow him, he couldn't move, not until he knew for sure that Shirlene wasn't in there.

Lorenzo had been gone a whole fifteen minutes before confirmation came. And when the building was finally cleared, when it was confirmed that there was no one inside, Israel's relief was short-lived. The fact that no one was inside the building didn't mean that things were okay. It didn't mean that Shirlene was safe. He'd been standing on the edge of relief when he took a quick step back into uncertainty. He was sure of three things in that moment: Shirlene wasn't in the building, but he also didn't know where Shirlene was; He knew where Chancey wasn't—at his house sleeping safely in his bed, and she wasn't at the crime scene; Lastly, he hadn't followed the man who could have possibly led him to both of them.

Satisfied by the *all clear* from the fire department, Israel got back in his car and drove home. He didn't have a plan, but he certainly had a purpose. He was going to find Lorenzo tonight. If it meant losing himself in the process, he didn't care. He was going to find him.

When he walked into his house, he could immediately sense that something was off. He didn't feel like there was danger, and he knew Lorenzo was too smart to come after him in his own home, but still, something wasn't right.

"Israel?"

From down his hallway came a soft whisper that felt something akin to a long-awaited breeze blowing through a cypress tree on a still, hot day. There came a voice from down his hallway that nearly took his breath away.

"Shirlene? Shirlene, that you? You okay?"

Overcome with relief as he rushed down the dark corridor to the room where just mere hours ago, he'd found so much joy, he walked in and was immediately struck with anguish. Even in the dark he could see the hurt in Shirlene's body. As he rushed over to her and got on his knees at the side of the bed, he gently touched her forehead with his thumb before kissing the top of her head.

"Shirlene, what happened? Who did this?"

"Lorenzo. He set my bar on fire, Israel. All I had to show for myself after all these years—he set it on fire."

In his forty-one years of living, Israel had never seen Shirlene cry, not once. And as her tears fell and rolled down her cheeks, his heart broke. "I'm gonna make this right, you hear me, Shirlene? I promise you, I'll make this right. I'm gonna find Lorenzo, I'm gonna find him, and I'm gonna put his ass in a box and set it on fire."

The sound of his heart breaking was drowned out by the sound of Shirlene's coughing as she choked on her own tears and residual smoke that was left in her lungs. Traumatized and angry, Israel gave her hand a gentle squeeze as her body shook from the coughing fit that her crying had sent her into. He took a breath and tried to put his own emotions aside. He kissed Shirlene's head before getting to his feet. "Hold on, Shirlene baby. I'm gonna get you some water. Hold on."

It took him less than a minute to get to the kitchen and get the water and get back to the bedroom. He began to kneel back down near Shirlene. He turned on the lamp that was on the nightstand by her head, and if it hadn't been for Shirlene's need of the water that he was holding in his hand, he'd have thrown the glass at the wall."

"Shirlene, your face . . ." Israel's head hung low as he shook it sorrowfully back and forth. "Don't tell me Lorenzo did this to you. Don't tell me that man beat you like this, Shirlene."

"Don't worry about it, Israel."

"Don't worry about it? Shirlene, your face, baby. When I get my hands on him, I swear—"

"Israel, listen to me. I've been through worse, and I'm still here. Don't worry about it. He ain't kill me. He ain't man enough to take me out. Don't worry about my face. You just go and find that girl. Find her before he does."

Shirlene's face was smudged with smoke, and her right eye was grossly swollen shut. Her lip was split, and her nose, if not broken, was definitely fractured. But the eye Shirlene could still open, the eye that did, it did the work of two. Her one good eye possessed so much intensity and conviction that it rendered the other eye unnecessary. Israel knew from the look that she gave him that what she said was not up for debate.

"He came to my bar around closing time trying to *interrogate* me." Shirlene huffed in disgust as she relived the night's events. "Tryna act all official at first like he was there on *police business*, but he knew that I knew better than that. That's when shit changed. That's when the real Lorenzo showed up and showed out. He started knocking glasses from off the top of my bar, started kicking stools over . . . and then he grabbed me. Grabbed me by my throat and said to me that he *knew*, he knew that I knew everything and so I better tell him something." Shirlene cleared her throat as she smiled to herself. "I ain't tell that rat bastard shit."

As Shirlene laughed, Israel couldn't help but laugh with her. "I know you didn't, Shirlene. Clearly, he ain't know who he was dealing with."

"Sure the hell didn't! But he learned tonight. Yes, he did." She frowned as she gave a firm nod of her head in agreement with her own statement. "Once he began to see he wasn't getting what he wanted, that's when he went on and threw a fit and started throwing my shit all over the damn place. And when he was through destroying my bar and tossing me around, that's when he knew, that's when he stopped and thought about you. I guess it dawned on the dumb son of a bitch that if you ain't know nothing about what he was doing before, you'd know it now. That's when he looked at me like I was a loose end. He sure the hell did . . . grabbed a bottle of my good vodka, tossed it across the room, lit a match, and threw it. Once the fire started, he knocked me upside my head one more time 'til I was down and then he left."

Israel's chest had doubled in size from the rage that had filled up inside of him as he sat and listened to Shirlene.

"Little did that fool know"—she pointed her finger as she turned her mouth up in disgust at the thought of

Lorenzo—"little did he know that the one he was looking for was out there looking for him too."

"Chancey?"

"Mm-hmm."

"Where is she, Shirlene?"

"Don't know. But five minutes after that fool left, I felt a hand reach out to me. She was there. She saw what he did, and she came in and got me off the floor and somehow and got me here. That little thing is a lot stronger than she looks."

"Don't I know it."

"He's still gonna kill her. You know it, I know it—and she knows it."

Israel's body went still. There was no arguing with the truth. It was a fact. Lorenzo was gonna kill Chancey when he found her. Israel's heart hurt. For the first time since he reentered his bedroom, he took his eyes off Shirlene and shut them so he could see Chancey's face, and once he could see her clearly, he exhaled. "I'm gonna do my best to see that, that doesn't happen."

Shirlene shook her head and sighed. "Love is always a losing game, baby. That's why I won't do it. The two of you—both of you willing to die for the other one. A losing game, I tell you. But, I did tell her before she left . . . I told her you would find her."

Israel desperately searched Shirlene's face for any sign of hope. He looked for any encouraging sign that he could grab hold of with both hands and hold on to, hope that perhaps she knew where Chancey was heading or hiding, hope that Shirlene could help him get to Chancey before Lorenzo could. But his hope was quickly dashed when he saw that Shirlene wouldn't look him in the eye. She would never stare him in the face and offer him that false promise, not with her words and not with her eyes.

"She said that she knew you'd come for her and that you might even find her, but that it would be too late by the time you did. She said she couldn't change her mind now, that it was too late. She wasn't gonna run away this time. She wouldn't take a single step back . . . that's how much she loves you."

In the silence that fell between them, Shirlene's pain in her body was overtaken by the fear in her heart and her fear of losing the man in front of her, the only family she had. That fear took up all the space in the room.

"I made you a promise years ago and you made one to me. I've never gone back on my word, Israel, but I feel like you about to go back on yours tonight. Promise me—I need to hear you say it again, one more time. Promise me you won't do nothing to get yourself killed."

He couldn't move. He couldn't speak either. He wasn't trying to get himself killed, but nevertheless, he was prepared to die.

As she reached out her hand to his, Shirlene sighed at his motionless body and nodded. Once she had her hand around his, she lifted Israel's hand to her bruised and busted lip and kissed it gently. *Nothing is dead and buried in New Orleans.* "That's what she said to me the first time I seen her. She had just arrived in New Orleans; it was a day or two before the corner store shooting. She walked into my bar from off the street 'cause she liked the look of the place from the outside, least that's what she said. Told me she was thinking 'bout moving down here from up North. I asked her why she'd wanna move down here; it seems so different than where she was coming from. And you know what she told me? She told me there were too many ghosts back home where she was from, too many ghosts and their souls were haunting her. She said she wanted to move here 'cause we don't bury our dead, and so we could never bury our truth and she liked the thought of that because that meant she couldn't be haunted by secrets and lies. If the dead wasn't buried, then neither was the truth—someone could always find the truth, someone would always know what happened." Shirlene paused and nodded her head in admiration. She may not have known Chancey well, but she was proud of her, prouder of her than she had ever been of herself. "And don't you know, she did. She found out who Lorenzo really is, what he's been doing, and where he's been doing it. Israel, she found Lorenzo's truth."

"How?"

"Don't know how she found it, but she came to me with the truth, because you told her that the truth was safe with me."

Shirlene sighed. The pain that she felt in that moment wasn't physical; it was emotional, and it wasn't for what she'd already been through but what she imagined lay ahead. "She's in the old, deserted church by Canal Street. It's the last of Lorenzo's stash houses she ain't burnt to the ground yet."

There was nothing left to say after that. Shirlene didn't want him to go, but she also knew he wouldn't stay. If she was in his place, she wouldn't have stayed either.

Without another word being spoken between them, Israel kissed Shirlene's forehead one final time before he got to his feet. After taking his badge out his pocket and throwing it on the nightstand, he grabbed his personal gun from the drawer, stuck an extra clip in his pocket along with his hunting knife, and he walked out the door.

CHAPTER TWENTY-FOUR

There was a sickening stench in the air that surrounded the old church, and the humidity of the night only added to the stink. The dark dilapidated building looked more menacing and ominous the closer Israel got to it. The quiet in the area was deafening, but he knew he wasn't alone. He couldn't see or hear anyone, but he knew they were there.

There weren't any signs on the property to stay out, no posted bills about trespassing or loitering. It was an abandoned church with forgotten graves behind it, death lingering in the air above and around it. It wasn't a place where anyone in their right mind would ever want to be, and yet the three were gathered there.

Walking through the front doors of the church would have been the quickest way to find Lorenzo, but it could have also been the quickest way to get himself shot. And while he didn't promise Shirlene, he wouldn't get himself killed. He certainly wasn't trying to make it happen, and he absolutely was not going to make it easy. Instead of walking up the steps to the front door, Israel walked around the side of the building toward the back.

Crouched down low with his shoulders and his back pressed against the side of the church, Israel let his head hang low so that he couldn't be seen through the stained-glassed windows above him as he slowly moved along the side of the building.

Just as he'd reached the last window before the turn that would lead him to the back door of the building, the sound of arrogance, stress, and anger came crashing down on his ears and echoed in his head.

"Did you really think that I didn't know it was you? Did you really think I didn't know that you were here? I run this city from the top to the bottom. This is my city. Nothing happens here that I don't know about."

He knew right away that the voice speaking was Lorenzo's, but it took him a minute to realize that Lorenzo wasn't talking to him. Israel stopped dead in his tracks as soon as he heard his voice. He was ready; he came ready. He was still crouched down low with his back against the side of the church, but he was ready to shoot. He had his finger on the trigger, and he was ready.

After a minute of waiting to hear footsteps, to hear the sound of any slight disturbance above him, Israel realized that the message he heard wasn't meant for him, which could only mean Lorenzo was talking to Chancey. Adrenaline shot through Israel's veins like lit gasoline. Anxiety and relief hit him all at once because he knew Lorenzo's babbling meant that Chancey was still alive.

"You know, I knew you were trouble the day I met you in the store and pulled your scrawny ass down out the ceiling. I should've shot you then."

Finally in the building, Israel took one careful step after the other and ensured that each move he made coincided with every threat that came out of Lorenzo's mouth. He moved each time that Lorenzo spoke and allowed Lorenzo's blustering arrogance to cover the sound of any squeak the floorboards made beneath him.

Once he'd made it to the end of the hallway, he was just a few yards away from his former partner. The only thing separating him from Lorenzo was the old wooden swinging door that led to the front of the church. The door that currently had them separated had a small glass window in it that Israel managed to peer through without being seen. Just beyond the choir pit, which was immediately on the other side of the door, and just past that, the pulpit, which even in the darkness looked dignified, Israel could see Lorenzo swaying back and forth between the pews at either side of him searching for Chancey. He was almost near the altar at the front of the church when Israel laid his palm softly on the door.

"So, what did she say to you that day? I saw the footage from before the shooting; she said something to you. What did she say?"

Lorenzo's ego led him down the aisle confidently. The sleeves of his blue button-up were rolled up to his elbows, his right arm extended with gun in hand, and his finger on the trigger. He was completely prepared to shoot everything and anything that moved.

"I tried to get it out of your friend—Otis, right? Yeah, Otis. I could tell he knew something too. There was this look he had. It was a look like, he knew something. I knew it as soon as I saw it. He knew, that I knew. But, he still wouldn't tell me anything. Not even after I stabbed him in the gut. He was lying there in pain, and I told him I would help him, gave him my word that I'd put him out of his misery; all he had to do was tell me what you told him . . . what I know you told him. But he wouldn't speak. So, I left him there to suffer—after I gave the knife a good twist of course, then I left. Left him there bleeding to death on the floor all alone."

Laughing to himself as he spoke, Lorenzo settled his gaze and his stance toward the left corner of the room where a broken-down organ sat. "That doesn't have to be you, Chancey." He laughed to himself again as he smiled at the darkness in front of him. "Oh, please don't misunderstand me; I'm still gonna kill you. But if you come out and tell me what I wanna know, I promise I'll do it quickly. No reason for you to suffer the way Otis did."

The sound of broken glass crunching beneath Israel's feet had given away his position before he could get as close as he wanted to. And as quickly as Lorenzo fired the first shot in his direction, Israel was able to sidestep into the abandoned choir pit at his side.

"Well, well, well, look who joined the party. Saint James! I was wondering if I would see you again this evening, Saint James."

Unamused and in no mood to entertain any conversation from his former partner, Israel peeked around the banister and fired a shot toward the sound of Lorenzo's voice.

"You shooting at me now, partner? Where's the love?"

Blinded by the darkness around him and anger inside of him, before Israel could see Lorenzo's face, he aimed his gun in the direction of Lorenzo's voice once against and leaned forward to glance around the banister, but before he could shoot, he saw the quick flash of fire from the muzzle of Lorenzo's gun as it went off. His shot just barely missed Israel's shoulder.

Pain and anger poured out of Lorenzo like a busted dam.

"Bitch!"

Lorenzo's shot had missed Israel because Chancey's blade had met its mark. From out of the darkness, she appeared just when Lorenzo became preoccupied with Israel and his focus was in the opposite direction. She'd crawled out from underneath one of the church pews behind Lorenzo, advanced quickly, and brought down her blade precisely. Chancey sliced open Lorenzo's arm like a butcher slicing the belly of a pig.

"You fucking bitch! You caught me off guard." Breathing heavy but still confident, Lorenzo chuckled. "I promise you this though. It won't happen again. That was your first and your last." Blood dripped from his arm, but the pain was overshadowed by the adrenaline he felt. Lorenzo whipped his body around, dropping his gun as he wrapped both his hands around Chancey's neck, lifting her off her feet as he violently shook her back and forth. He laughed as he abruptly dropped her to the ground, snatched her blade from her, and held it to her neck. "Is this what you came for, partner?"

Gun drawn and aimed at Lorenzo's head, Israel stepped out from the choir pit and made his way to the altar.

With one hand clamped firmly around Chancey's tiny neck, Lorenzo pulled her off the ground and to her feet, holding the blade to her neck while he laughed. "She's right here, brother. Come get her."

Israel slowly advanced toward Lorenzo. He glanced down at the gun Lorenzo had dropped in the aisle when Chancey had taken him by surprise.

"Don't worry about that. I don't even need it." Without hesitation or humility, Lorenzo moved forward, stepped on the gun in front of him, and slid it to the side underneath one of the pews.

"Now you, brother. Put it down and come get your girl."

"Just shoot him, Israel. Chancey's soft voice was steady and reassuring as she pulled at Lorenzo's forearm. "It's okay, Israel. I'll be okay. Just shoot him."

"He ain't that good a shot, sweetheart. Between the two of us, I was always the better cop." As he felt her struggle in his arms trying to free herself, Lorenzo laughed as he tightened his grip around Chancey's throat.

"Here, let me give you some incentive."

In a flash, the blade that was once at Chancey's neck was lowered and was now in her side. Lorenzo smiled as he quickly brought the bloody blade back up to Chancey's jugular. "How 'bout now? You gonna come get her now?"

The sound of Chancey's scream as Lorenzo stabbed her sent ice water through Israel's veins and nearly stopped his heart.

"Don't do it, Israel." Bleeding profusely, struggling to breathe, and on the edge of passing out, Chancey fought to stay on her feet. She could see it in Israel's body language, and she knew that he was prepared to lay his gun down and try to get to her, so she fought off unconsciousness to try and prevent that from happening. "I'm dead already, Israel, you know that. Just shoot him. It's okay. I love you. I forgive you. I'll be okay. I promise."

"Shut up! Enough!" As Lorenzo pressed the blade harder against Chancey's skin until blood began to bead up and trickle down her neck, Lorenzo took a small step forward toward Israel, dragging Chancey with him as his human shield. "Put it down and come get your girl."

The soft yellow light from the broken window was just enough for Israel to see blood dripping down Chancey's neck. Enraged, he winced as he looked at her sad eyes, before quickly casting his gun aside and charging at Lorenzo.

After throwing Chancey to the floor, Lorenzo repositioned the knife in his hand and smiled. "Yeah, come get some, partner."

As quickly as he had cast aside his gun, his hunting knife was in his hand. As he lunged at Lorenzo, the tip of his blade caught Lorenzo's jaw, causing bright red blood to spatter across his wet white T-shirt.

But Lorenzo hadn't missed either, and not all the blood on Israel's shirt was that of his opponent. Israel's own blood was now seeping through his shirt from where Lorenzo had caught him, right above his rib cage. On his right side.

While Lorenzo hadn't brought his own knife to this fight, he was more than happy to use the one he had. He was enjoying the close-contact combat. A few more jabs between them, each of them missing the other ever so slightly, the thrill of the duel got the better of Lorenzo, and while he was caught up in the thrill of things, he missed when Israel switched hands with the blade and was shocked when he came in hard and fast with a right hook, which landed directly on Lorenzo's eye.

Stunned, Lorenzo charged at Israel, swinging with his left arm and kicking with his right leg. In the midst of trying to kick Israel's legs from out underneath him, he exposed his arm just enough for Israel to take a slice out of it, adding to the gash that Chancey had given him early, briefly exposing the white meat of his forearm before it quickly became consumed with blood. As the pain radiated up and down his arm, the distraction gave Israel just enough time to pry the knife out of Lorenzo's hand.

Between the two of them, Lorenzo had always been the one with the physical upper hand. He had never questioned his success in a hand-to-hand fight with Israel. The fact that it was taking this long to put Israel down was beginning to irritate him. As frustration began to pour out of him, Lorenzo took a cheap shot at Israel, kicking him in the groin and causing him to briefly double over in pain. While Israel tried to reclaim his senses, Lorenzo capitalized on the moment and went at him with both fist, landing blow after blow against Israel's face.

While he expected more integrity in a fight between the two of them, Israel wasn't too shocked that Lorenzo took the cowardly route and kicked him between the legs. As he tried to quickly recover from the unexpected pain, once he could get himself upright again, Israel advanced toward Lorenzo with knives in both hands. He used the butt of his hunting knife in combination with his fist to strike Lorenzo in the head again and again and again . As Lorenzo tried to defend himself with his injured arm, he sank down to the floor, and as he did—when it appeared that Israel had bested Lorenzo— for the briefest moment, Israel paused to look over at where Chancey had fallen . It was in that moment that Lorenzo found just the time he needed to quickly reach forward and grab the gun that he had previously kicked aside.

Silence fell down on the room like a curtain. It felt as if the moon had suddenly dropped right out of the sky. The air seemed cooler and the night suddenly seemed darker. The two men faced each other, each one huffing and puffing trying to catch their breath as the adrenaline continued to pump intensely within their veins. Israel stood his ground next to Chancey, while Lorenzo aimed the gun at him and slowly backed up until he got to a place where he felt he was in the clear to get back onto his feet.

"It didn't have to end this way, partner. I used to think that maybe one day you and I could do business together the same way me and Vic did. But I should have known that it wouldn't work out. I mean, it didn't work out for Vic, right?"

Israel balled his fists at his sides as he stared back at Lorenzo. "So, you *did* kill Victoria?"

"Well, I didn't pull the trigger, but yeah. I did what I had to do. Crazy bitch had a baby and lost her mind. She was jeopardizing my entire operation."

"And the other people in the store that day?"

Lorenzo shrugged as he turned his mouth up at the insinuation that he should feel remorse. "Casualties of war."

"Casualties of war? You're a fucking coward. Go ahead and pull the trigger." Lifting his hand to his heart, Israel patted his chest as he firmly nodded at Lorenzo. "Go ahead take your shot. And you better not miss 'cause I'm coming for you if you do."

"I won't."

"No!" With the last bit of strength she had, Chancey pulled herself from off the floor and flung herself into Israel's arms and caught a bullet in her back, the same bullet that was meant for Israel's heart.

Shot fired, and now filled with the feeling of satisfaction and amusement, Lorenzo laughed and smacked the pew next to him with pure glee before he turned around and quickly and ran out the front door.

With his arms wrapped around her waist and her arms hanging loosely around his neck, as her head lay against the space between his chin and his chest, for a brief moment it was as if they were merely embracing one another. If he hadn't heard the shot, he would never have believed that she was dying in his arms.

As her head began to fall and her body began to go limp in his arms, he reluctantly came to terms with the truth of the situation. He slowly lowered himself to the floor and held on to Chancey firmly. He felt empty. Holding on to her was the only thing keeping him from losing his mind.

"Chancey, don't."

Kneeling on the floor, cradling her in a way that he hoped would coax her heart to continue to keep beating, Chancey looked up at him and smiled as best she could. "I love you, Israel. Don't let him win. Don't let him get away."

When her eyes shut, Israel's heart broke. Twice she'd saved him that night, traded her life for his. He would do this for her. He would find Lorenzo; he wouldn't let him get away. As he softly touched his hand against her cheek, he bent down and kissed her lips one final time before laying her down carefully on the floor. Back on his feet, as he looked down at her one last time, there was a moment of sorrow he felt that was so intense it nearly crippled him. After shaking off the shock, Israel found his strength—he found it in all the tears he could not cry in that moment. Keeping that soul-crushing sorrow at bay gave him the conviction he needed to do what he had promised, and so he headed out the front doors of the church in pursuit of Lorenzo.

It was near dawn when he walked out the church. He'd gotten into his car without knowing where he was going. The only thing he knew in that moment was that he had to get to Lorenzo and finish things so that he could get back to Chancey.

He hadn't been driving for more than five minutes before he looked behind him in his rearview mirror and saw lights. Within seconds, one cop car had turned into ten . His car was surrounded, and all guns were aimed at him.

CHAPTER TWENTY-FIVE

It had been three weeks since Shirlene's bar had been set on fire, three weeks after Israel felt Chancey's body go limp in his arm. It had been three weeks since Israel had been a free man. It had been three weeks since the world had made sense to him, or that anything mattered to him. Nothing mattered anymore, nothing except the fact that he never made it back to her that night; he never got a chance to say his final goodbye to the love of his life.

Immediately following the showdown between him and Lorenzo, Israel was taken into custody and was labeled as a dirty cop. He'd been labeled a drug dealer and a murderer—none of which mattered to him, nothing mattered to him. Israel didn't have a plan after he left the church that evening three weeks back and went after Lorenzo, but much to his dismay and surprise, Lorenzo did have a plan. More than just a little bit of evidence was found against Israel. Evidence was found against Israel that tied him to crimes he didn't even know had been committed.

When he was asked to give a statement, he didn't provide one; he didn't see the point. To every question he was asked, his only response was, "Did you find her yet?"

He couldn't make it back to Chancey that evening, but he was insistent that someone did. Two units went back to the church while Israel sat in an interrogation room the night of his arrest, but both units came back with the same response: There was no one there. There was no one at the church dead or alive. The absence of Chancey's body compounded with the false evidence Lorenzo had created against him. It all made things look really bad for Israel, really bad. But as bleak as things were, he didn't care. He didn't care about the charges against him, his ruined reputation amongst his peers, or his freedom being taken away from him. The only thing that mattered to him was her, and she was gone.

The guards at the jail where he was being held had already judged and convicted him before a jury had even been selected for his trial. They taunted him and treated him like trash. He was only let out of his cell twice a day for recreation, and when the time came, he was always brought out late and put back in early. His food tray had been shoved through his door so hard that it often fell to the floor inside his cell and went to waste. But Israel took it all in silently. All the mistreatment, all the gossip, and sideways glances, he took it all and remained unmoved by any of it. His indifference toward his jailers infuriated the guards even more. They took his sadness as arrogance and his heartbreak as a lack of remorse.

After three weeks of limited human interaction, barely eating, and hardly washing, Israel had his first visitor.

Inside the crowded visitation room, Israel looked around as his cuffs were being removed. He was curious to see who had shown up to see him. He didn't have to look too long. Joy immediately filled his heart when his eyes found hers, and his heart jumped.

"Ms. Shirlene."

"Hey, my baby."

Wrapping his arms around Shirlene and hugging her felt like coming home. "What you doing here, Ms. Shirlene?"

"You know I had to come down here and check on you."

"You shouldn't be here. You know how people talk. I don't want him coming after you again."

"Let him come."

Israel smiled and nodded. There was no use arguing. Shirlene had never let anyone intimidate her, and Israel knew she wasn't about to start now.

"You look good, Shirlene. I'm glad to see you this way."

"Can't say the same about you now, can I?"

Israel lowered his head and shut his eyes. "No, I suppose you can't."

"He ain't won yet, baby. He might think he did, but I'm here to shame the devil and tell you the truth . . . he ain't won shit. You won't be in here long either, I promise you that."

"Shirlene, I don't want you putting yourself in danger for me. I'm okay."

"The hell you are." Shirlene took a quick look around the room before tapping on the table to get Israel's attention. "You still trust me, don't you?"

"Yes, ma'am. With my life."

"Then trust me now, Israel Saint James. I give you my word, he will not win, and you will get out of here."

He trusted Shirlene, he hadn't lied about that, but her words in that moment, her promise left him with an empty feeling. "Any word about Chancey?"

Shirlene sighed as she shook her head. "No. Not a trace of her. Her body is evidence against him. It's not likely we'll ever find her." Shirlene paused as she raised her eyebrows and pursed her lips together. "But like Chancey said, 'We don't bury our dead.' Lorenzo ain't gonna be able to bury the truth."

"I'd drink to that, if I could."

"And you will, baby. You will."

"I don't know how to explain it, but she made me feel whole. Never been more at peace in my life than when I was just lying next to her."

"I know what you mean. The Quarter has always been the love of my life, and now it just don't feel the same. It feels broken, like it's missing something. It's a Quarter short compassion—my love has lost its heart."

***

Three weeks after his visit with Shirlene, Israel was once again advised that he had a visitor. Unfortunately, it wasn't anyone he wanted to see. He made an effort to decline the visit, but the guard escorting him insisted he take a seat.

"Saint James. Good to see you, buddy." Lorenzo sat across from him perfectly postured, broad shouldered, and smiling from ear to ear.

"What do you want?"

"I came to check on you. Make sure they treating you all right in here. You still in protective custody? I hope so 'cause you know things can get bad for a cop out there in general population."

"So now you care about me, huh?" Israel huffed as he glared at Lorenzo's cocky smiling face. "You care about me the same way you cared about Victoria, right?"

Lorenzo chuckled as he stretched back in his seat. "Vic is dead and buried, Saint James. Leave the dead alone. Let her lay."

A sudden sparkle hit Israel's eyes as he raised an eyebrow and looked back at Lorenzo. "We don't bury our dead here in New Orleans." It was then that he saw her. He could see Chancey's face as clearly as he could see Lorenzo sitting across from him. She was looking up at him smiling. Her hands were wrapped around his neck, and then like a bad dream he could feel the rush her of warm blood coating his fingers.

Despite his best efforts to make this visit seem like it was one rooted in concern, Lorenzo was beginning to grow impatient. After looking around the room and giving a casual nod to some of the guards that were posted in various corners of the room, he looked back at Israel and shook his head feigning dismay.

"Can't believe it's come to this, Saint James. You being in here, it's a tragedy, a real fucking tragedy. I wish you would have reached out if you were in trouble. I could have helped you. You were a good detective once upon a time. It kills me to see you like this."

"*I'll kill you.*"

Lorenzo smirked at the comment but decided not to address it. He was putting on a show, and this scene wasn't finished yet. "The boys back at the station are all pretty upset. I told them not to be too hard on you, that you was probably just trying to help out Shirlene and just got in over your head." Lorenzo spoke loud enough for people struggling to listen to hear everything he was saying, but low enough to give off the appearance that his conversation was meant for Israel alone. "I tried to tell you that women wasn't no good and she'd turn on you. Now look, you're in here and she's in the wind. Do yourself a favor and tell me where she is so I can go talk to her for you."

Israel couldn't help but chuckle a little. If Lorenzo was here looking for Shirlene, then that meant she was staying true to her word, which Israel hadn't doubted for a minute. He just hadn't expected her to be so quick about it. He knew she would do anything and everything to get him out of jail, and based on today's events, what she was doing was making trouble for Lorenzo, so much so that he'd come looking to him to help find her.

Annoyed by Israel's audacity to laugh in his face, Lorenzo slapped the table. "Hey, this ain't a joke. Tell me how to find her before *someone* else ends up dead."

The sound of his hand slapping the table sounded like a gun firing in Israel's ear, and once again he saw Chancey, he saw her falling into his arms, and he could almost hear the sound of her voice; it came to him like a faraway whisper echoing in his ears, *"Israel, I love you."* When the moment passed, in a sudden fit of rage, Israel jumped across the table and wrapped his hands around Lorenzo's neck. The force of his lunge knocked Lorenzo out of his seat and onto his back on the floor. It took five guards to pull Israel off Lorenzo that day.

***

It had been almost two weeks since Israel had almost choked Lorenzo to death in the visitation room, and Israel was finally being released from solitary confinement. He didn't bother to defend or justify his actions when the jail staff had questioned him. They didn't care what he had to say, and he didn't care to say anything. The hearing was a formality. He expected to receive the harshest punishment for what he'd done, and that's what they gave him. What he hadn't expected, though, was that they would be releasing him into the general population. Lorenzo was long gone and unlikely to return for another a visit, but he'd left Israel a message, a message that had been delivered and Israel had received it. Lorenzo wanted him dead, and he found people to help him get the job done.

After a much-needed shower, on his first day in his new cell Israel looked at himself in the distorted carnival-like mirror and rubbed the stubble on his face as he thought about the losses he'd endured throughout the course of his life, and he sighed as he questioned what it was all for. Was everything he'd gone through, everything he'd given up and gotten over, was everything he sacrificed for, sweat for and bled for—was it worth it?

The sound of the lock on his cell door being opened brought him back to his senses. With the long series of unfortunate events that had plagued his life still playing in his mind, he walked outside to the yard and held his face up toward the sun. The shining sun and Louisiana heat were a comfort to him in that moment. Peace seemed well beyond his reach, but there was a certain relief he felt as he stood alone in the yard surrounded by distrust and danger.

He began to slowly and thoughtfully walk the perimeter of the yard and was mindful not to encroach upon any of the spaces that were already occupied. As he walked along fence line furthest from the building, he noticed a group of inmates were beginning to approach him. Two of the guards who had previously escorted him on visits were at the back of the group speaking with one of the inmates, who Israel could only imagine was the one *in charge* of the small gang that was now just a few feet away from him. When they reached where he stood, they didn't waste any time talking; there wasn't anything to say. This wasn't their fight, yet they threw punches at him all the same.

One man against ten, Israel didn't stand a chance. The other inmates went after him two and three at a time, attacking him from all angles. His eye was nearly swollen shut, his lip was busted, and blood was steadily streaming from his nose, but Israel would not back down. He kept fighting. At some point during the assault, he'd been knocked down and was on one knee struggling to get back to his feet when he suddenly felt a hand fall on his shoulder. Much to his surprise and relief, the hand he felt wasn't hostile.

After quickly glancing at the fingers that firmly gripped his shoulder, Israel exhaled, and then from the corner of his swollen eye he looked back over to his attackers. Much to his confusion, he could see the ten inmates who had just attacked him slowly retreating. Once again, to his surprise and overwhelming joy, there was suddenly another hand on his shoulder, this time on his left side, and that hand that held him firmly and steadied him, and then together the two men at either side of him helped him to his feet.

Standing tall once again, with both his feet planted firmly on the ground, Israel took a deep breath, and it was like he could taste the change in the atmosphere. He knew without looking that the man to the left of him, as well as the one on his right, meant him no harm. Not only that, but he knew that they were standing *with* him, and that knowledge gave him strength; their grace and their mercy made him strong. What he hadn't known, what he had to turn around and see was that almost half of the inmates in the yard had come over to where he was losing the fight for his life; they had all come and stood behind him. Faces from old cases he worked, faces from his old neighborhood, they all came from various areas across the yard and they stood with him. They stood in silence, and not a single word was spoken, but their message was clear: Israel was not alone.

An overwhelming sense of pride filled Israel as he stood there with the men. He glanced over at the officers who had been watching and who had encouraged the brutal attack on him, and as he took the back of his hand to wipe the blood from his mouth, he nodded at them and then watched the ten inmates who attacked him all lower their eyes and walk away.

CHAPTER TWENTY-SIX

Tuesday morning, after two and a half months in jail, today was the first day of Israel's trial. Standing in his cell wearing khakis that were two sizes too big and a blue button-up shirt that fit a little too snug, Israel prepared himself to walk into court and give his statement.

As he looked in the mirror at himself and thought about the losses in his life once again, he smiled at himself because he had concluded that, yes they were worth it, that the large majority of everything he'd endured was worth it. The struggles he faced and the sacrifices he made were all worth it. His heart, his actions, and his integrity spoke for him so loudly that men he'd taken away from their families, men who had lost their freedom because he did his job, these men, they all came to his defense when he was down, and they pulled him back up. The respect and admiration he had earned was something that could never be taken from him. To know he was worthy of it gave him so much joy. He looked at his reflection—his black eye, busted lip, and bruised jaw—and he nodded. "Bruised but not broken."

Thankfully his ride from the jail to the courthouse was brief. The animosity that came radiating off the guards that sat up front in the inmate transport van overpowered the air conditioner in the vehicle and made the air inside stuffy and uncomfortable. Despite the unpleasant atmosphere, he smiled at the irony. They'd already condemned him; the ones who were supposed to uphold the law and find the truth, according to them he was already guilty. It was the ones with the sordid pasts, the *guilty* themselves, the already convicted, the cons, and the ones on the *wrong* side of the law that would see him free and help fight for the truth to be told.

As he entered the side door that led to the courtroom, he was immediately overwhelmed by the crowd that had turned out and was sitting in the gallery. Behind the prosecutor sat Lorenzo, and with him were a few of his former colleagues. None of these men would look him in the eye. They sat in opposition of him. These men he once called friends and treated like family turned their heads when he walked in, but Israel was unfazed. He was a little surprised at first, but he knew when he saw them and saw how they refused to see him. He knew in that moment that although he was the one on trial, his integrity and his pride were very much intact and he wouldn't be shrinking for anyone that day no matter where he sat.

On the defense side, his side of the room, Shirlene sat right up front and was seated right behind where Israel would be seated. Much to his surprise, sitting right next to Shirlene, was Baby Ruth Ann, and next to her was Victoria's training officer, retired Detective LaGrange. Beside LaGrange and behind him sat several patrol officers who walked the streets that Israel loved.

When he was close enough to her and the guards had removed the cuffs, Shirlene reached out and held Israel's arm as she gently touched the side of his bruised face and shook her head.

"I'm still standing, Shirlene. I'm okay." And he was. Israel was okay. In that moment he was better than okay. He hadn't reached out to anyone for help, but help had shown up all the same. In the midst of his darkest hour, the light and the grace that he had given to others over the years was there today in that room. Today, the day he was prepared to speak for himself, all his work, all his acts of kindness, generosity, and mercy he'd extended to the people inside and outside of his neighborhood, they showed up for him and they were all prepared to speak for him. He was not alone.

The prosecution had taken the morning. They had a lot of circumstantial evidence, and two witnesses Israel had never seen before, and their key witness of course, Lorenzo, who put on quite a performance. Lorenzo's self-sacrificing testimony was an exceptional work of fiction that had some of the jury members eyeing Israel with a small degree of contempt. When he stepped down from the witness box, he was so proud of himself he couldn't help but smile.

But the afternoon, those p.m. hours, they belonged to the defense. The judge and the jury listened intently to the statements made by the defenses witnesses, and as they spoke, the prosecution began to sweat. The prosecution had the witness list but had concluded that the names listed would only be speaking to character not fact. The prosecutor was wrong. He was unprepared, caught off guard, and just all around wrong. His case was not as open and shut as he thought it would be, despite having Lorenzo's sworn statement. The prosecutor had tried to paint Israel as a man without honor, a crooked cop whose integrity lay with the streets he grew up in, the same streets that corrupted him and made him turn his back on his brothers in blue.

Lorenzo wasn't surprised by Shirlene's presence or her testimony, and he'd worked with the prosecutor at length on how to discredit her. What he hadn't anticipated was the sworn testimony of Baby Ruth Ann, which was backed up by Victoria's training officer.

Once he knew for sure Ruth Ann was testifying, Lorenzo expected her to accuse him of stealing and selling drugs—a statement he was fully prepared to discredit by using her own history of drug use and arrest against her. But the testimony she gave was not one he foresaw, and what made it worse was that she had someone to cosign her truth. She had someone more respected and more widely loved than Lorenzo could ever hope to be. Both Baby Ruth and former Detective LaGrange testified to the fact that Victoria was terrified of Lorenzo. He stated that, while once upon a time she may have been a good officer and may have been an even a better detective, she lost herself and what she stood for when she got involved with Lorenzo. Additionally, it was her sister, Baby Ruth Ann, who offered her a way out and an opportunity to get away from Lorenzo.

After Lorenzo and Victoria had ended their relationship, he'd gotten involved with Baby Ruth. He'd let her off on minor violations in exchange for information and other more salacious requests. Eventually, Baby Ruth ended up pregnant and came clean to Victoria about what was going on, and Victoria, who had just gotten into a relationship with someone new, saw Baby Ruth's unfortunate situation as an opportunity to get out of the unit she was in and far away from Lorenzo. Victoria faked her pregnancy. She was never pregnant, she didn't have a baby, Ruth Ann did, but by pretending she was pregnant she was able to switch departments and stay off the streets and get the one thing she wanted most of all, which was to be away from Lorenzo. When Baby Ruth gave birth, she delivered at home. For Victoria, it was the perfect plan. A baby was coming no matter what, and Baby Ruth was trying to get clean, and she couldn't handle a baby and sobriety at the same time. Also, Victoria needed a way out of where she was that could be understood and not questioned, and a baby would have given her just that. What Baby Ruth couldn't handle and take on, Victoria needed to start her new life. In spite of how he was conceived, Baby Ruth loved her son, and she didn't want Lorenzo to have anything to do with him, so she gave her son over with love to her sister to raise and keep safe and, most importantly, keep away from Lorenzo.

Baby Ruth also testified that the night of the car crash when the drugs went missing and the car caught on fire, there was at least fifty thousand dollars of stolen drugs in the vehicle, which she had taken from her former dealer. She swore that the drugs had not been in the fire. She swore that the drugs she stole had in fact been stolen from her that same day. She testified that this incident was the one that made Victoria change her life and want to get away from Lorenzo. It was Victoria who had told Lorenzo about the drugs, and it was Lorenzo who stole them from Baby Ruth. Victoria nearly cost her sister her life telling Lorenzo that information, and she felt terrible for doing so, but what she couldn't live with was the lives she stole because of the drugs Lorenzo had to have. Victoria had accused three men who had nothing to do with the incident of drug trafficking. They were all arrested and sent to prison, where one of the innocent men died while she covered up the truth.

After a few months had gone by, and with her guilt getting the best of her, Victoria sought out LaGrange's council. She told him her truth and asked how she could possibly make things right now. His advice was to get away from the situation but leave a trail that led back to Lorenzo so that someone else could say the things she couldn't. So that's exactly what she did. That day in the store when Lorenzo sent his hired help to kill her, she told Chancey everything, and Chancey told Shirlene, and Shirlene told the court.

That afternoon, former Detective LaGrange gave credit to two witness the prosecution had labeled corrupt and not credible, and he did so based on the testimony of a man who had lied and conspired against everyone. The jury's eyes had been opened, and now they all blazed with contempt and their glares all fell on Lorenzo.

As LaGrange spoke, Shirlene sat behind Israel, nodding intently at the prosecutor and softly mumbling to herself. "Uh-huh, tell me my statement can't be trusted and you over there cosigning lies. We got the truth over here."

After LaGrange had given his testimony, two of the patrol cops in the gallery took the stand and testified to what they'd seen and heard around the city. None of what they testified to spoke kindly of Lorenzo. Israel may have not known these men, but these men knew the truth, and they spoke loudly and without hesitation and everything they said was to Israel's credit.

Retired Chief of Police Baptiste was the last to take the stand of the people currently seated on the defense's side. Baptiste had served the city and its people for decades. His work and his conduct were beyond reproach. That afternoon, Retired Chief of Police Baptiste characterized Israel as one of the best men he had the pleasure to know. He swore under God that Israel Saint James was a true friend with a lion's heart and it was his honor to know him. He likened Israel to a calm and steady place in any storm, and he surmised that he believed with all his heart that Israel would drown if it meant helping someone else out of troubled water. In short, Baptiste stood with Detective Israel Saint James that day and would stand with him every single day going forward.

After Baptiste spoke, two of the three men who had been sitting by Lorenzo got up and left the courtroom. It wasn't until the three men left that Israel had looked over to the prosecution's side of the room and realized that half the people who were sitting there when he walked in had silently taken their leave throughout the defense's testimony.

As the proceedings began to die down and Israel was preparing to take the stand in his own defense, his attorney rose and informed the court that his confidential informant had just arrived in the building. Before the prosecution could object, the courtroom doors opened and an officer that Israel had never seen before walked in. As the officer approached the witness stand, Israel's attorney introduced him to the court as United States Marshall Eugene Lee. As Special Agent Lee took the stand and raised his hand to be sworn in, the doors to the court opened again and the soft sound of metal tapping against the linoleum filled the room. The sound came from the crutch that helped to support her weight since she had not yet fully recovered from her injuries. The sound was made by Chancey Morris as she slowly and confidently entered the room with her head held high and a grin on her lips.

All talking in the courtroom ceased, and everyone watched in silent suspense as both Israel and Lorenzo shot to their feet.

"Object! Object now!" Lorenzo's fearless façade quickly faded as Chancey made her way to the front row of the gallery and took her place beside Shirlene—behind Israel.

The prosecution objected and asked to approach the bench. They didn't object because Lorenzo insisted that they should; the prosecution objected because they were clearly confused and already at their wits end after everything that had transpired throughout the course of the day. The prosecutor argued to the judge that Eugene should not be heard because he had yet to be vetted as a credible witness, to which the judge responded that was what cross-examination was for. Additionally, the prosecution asserted that aside from a character reference, which they felt would just be time consuming and unnecessary, there was no evidence that Special Agent Lee could present that would strengthen the defense's case or be relevant at all.

Overhearing the conversation, Eugene looked at the judge and smiled as he nodded toward Chancey, and then looked at the prosecutor confidently. "My evidence."

Still standing, Israel stared at Chancey in complete shock. Being able to stand in front of her and see her smile again was like breathing clean air for the first time. "You're here."

Chancey smiled as she set her crutches aside and allowed them to rest against the banister. "Even if I could have run, I wouldn't have."

Shirlene laughed as she looked over at Lorenzo. She found a great deal of enjoyment in how distressed he looked. "Ha! The dead has arisen, and the truth is gonna set my baby free today."

Chancey placed her hand over Israel's heart and nodded. "I'm here. I'm sorry I kept you waiting so long, but I'm here now and I promise—I'm not going anywhere. You are not alone."

As he held his hand over the top of hers, Israel exhaled deeply as the tears his eyes were unable to cry for two months came rushing down his face. He barely heard the judge when he ruled that the case had been dismissed. There was an uproar in the courtroom as the gavel fell, but in the space between them there was calm and quiet, and Israel's heart was full as he looked back at Chancey and nodded. "'Till my heart stopped beating . . . I would wait for you forever, Chance. Always."